Angel By My Side

AMELIA'S STORY

Other Avon Camelot Books in the
ANGEL BY MY SIDE *Trilogy by*
Erin Flanagan
Coming Soon

LILY'S STORY
GRACE'S STORY

Angel By My Side

AMELIA'S STORY

ERIN FLANAGAN

AN AVON CAMELOT BOOK

ANGEL BY MY SIDE: AMELIA'S STORY is an original publication of Avon Books. This work has never before appeared in book form.

AVON BOOKS
A division of
The Hearst Corporation
1350 Avenue of the Americas
New York, New York 10019

Copyright © 1995 by Erin Flanagan
Published by arrangement with the author
Library of Congress Catalog Card Number: 94-96805
ISBN: 0-380-78215-4
RL: 4.8

First Avon Camelot Printing: July 1995

CAMELOT TRADEMARK REG. U.S. PAT. OFF. AND IN OTHER COUNTRIES, MARCA REGISTRADA, HECHO EN U.S.A.

Printed in the U.S.A.

OPM   10 9 8 7 6 5 4 3 2 1

To Robert and Mark,
my almost angels

Angel By My Side

AMELIA'S STORY

Ahhh. Field trips. The best thing about school! I smiled and looked out the school bus window as we passed the corner of Hollywood and Vine.

Our bus stopped at the giant pagoda of Mann's Chinese Theatre, home of one of Southern California's most famous tourist attractions: See your favorite movie stars' foot and hand prints in cement! Try them on for size!

I tried, unsuccessfully, to fit my feet into various imprints. Then I found a perfect fit.

"Oh, great!" I sighed. "Look at this, Shura. My feet fit into Clark Gable's footprints!"

"Mine fit into Marilyn Monroe's. Amelia, why do people do this anyway? Who'd want to stick their hands and feet in cement?"

"I wouldn't mind! Only really famous people get

their imprints here. Of course, *my* feet would fit into Gable's! I can't believe this, I'm not even thirteen yet, and I have the same size feet as a grown man. Now I kind of wish we hadn't come here."

"At least we're not in school." She knelt and tried to fit her hands into Monroe's imprints. "Hey, look at that, my big Russian paws are humongous compared to her dainty, little pinkies. Come on, let's go try on some other prints."

I nodded and followed my best friend, Shura Najinsky, as she suddenly took off across the sun-drenched slabs of imprinted cement.

"Don't tell anybody about where my feet fit, Shura. Okay?"

"Come on. Who would I tell? Besides, nobody cares. They're just feet." She pinned an unruly, black braid back into place and tried to wedge her feet into Elizabeth Taylor's footprints.

"Sure, just feet to you. You wear a nice, reasonable size seven and a half, while I flap around in size ten! I should order my shoes from the clown catalogue."

"I've heard this already. You hate your feet, and your hair, and your thighs, and your complexion, and your skinny legs—"

"Okay, okay, I get it. I want to improve myself, that's all. I want to look like a model, instead of a—"

"You read too many *Seventeen* magazines."

My face flushed and I put my hands on my hips. "Well, I happen to like *Seventeen!*"

I spent many dull weekends poring over the magazine: the advice, the new fashions, and the makeup tips.

"Good thing you like it so much. They need people to buy into their plastic version of pretty, so they can sell the stupid magazine."

"Whatever," I said with a shrug. Pretty was pretty. Did it really matter so much if it was plastic?

She elbowed me. "Hey, look across the courtyard. Old Wats is caught in that clump of Japanese tourists. This is my chance; I'm going inside this mausoleum of a theater and find a bathroom."

"Maybe you better not. Mrs. Watson said this morning before we left that we couldn't go running around inside anywhere without permission."

Shura shook off my concern with a laugh. "What are they going to do, arrest me for peeing?"

"They'll get mad."

"BFD."

That was her favorite phrase, BFD. Shura told her mother it stands for big, furry deal; but it doesn't.

"They can't stop me from needing to pee. Besides, if they tried, my mother would go to the school and yell at them in Russian. They'll want to avoid *that*." She grinned and marched right into the theater.

As I watched her storm the bathroom, I realized how different Shura was from everyone else in our school; like a sunflower blooming in a neat row of carrots.

The first time I saw Shura was when I went to kindergarten. She came into the room with her mother and they talked quietly in Russian while they waited to see the teacher. Right away some kids started making fun of Mrs. Najinsky because of her dark, heavy clothes, and her funny accent. Shura understood more English than her mother so she walked over to the table, picked up a big bucket of crayons, and hit the loudest kid right in the mouth with it. "Close your mean mouth. You are bad boy!" she declared, with braids askew and fists clenched.

I'd been her best friend ever since. Ugly ducklings always recognize the swans.

The *squeep* of Mrs. Watson's whistle jerked me back to the present. She freed herself from the tourists and fanned herself with a map. Every time she fanned, the skin under her upper arm jiggled with the effort. Kids at school called them "Watson's bat wings," and I felt bad for her whenever they said it because I kind of liked her. She always smelled like school—that funny mixture of chalk, sweat, and freshly ground pencils.

4

"Oh, my goodness! Such a crowd," she said, clutching her whistle necklace. "Class! That was the ten minute warning! Our next stop is The La Brea Tar Pits, then the Los Angeles County Museum of Art. Back to the bus in exactly ten minutes, and stay out of that gift shop, this is not a shopping expedition!"

I strolled over to John Wayne's footprints and almost put my feet in, but didn't dare—they'd probably be bigger than his!

Mrs. Watson materialized at my elbow. "Having a nice time, Amelia?"

"Oh, yes, I am. This is pretty cool for a field trip. I love old movies and old movie stars and stuff."

When she smiled I noticed lipstick smeared on her front tooth. "Have you matched your feet with anyone famous yet?" she asked.

"Ah, well, not really." No way was I going to own up to Clark Gable's shoe size!

"My feet matched Mary Pickford's," she said. "She was America's Sweetheart, you know. Back in the days of silent films."

"Sure, I know about her. She married an actor named Douglas Fairbanks and they were the first really big movie stars we had."

"My, my, my." Mrs. Watson stared at me from behind thick glasses. Her watery blue eyes looked interested. "How on earth do you know about that ancient Hollywood history?"

"I read some books about the early days of Hollywood. I mean, since we live here and everything . . ." I left out the part about wanting to be an actress.

Mrs. Watson leaned toward me conspiratorially. "I took the tour of stars' homes once, when I was a little girl, and I saw their mansion, Pickfair. I even got a glimpse of Mary, leaving in her chauffeur-driven car."

"Really?"

"Oh, yes, and it was so exciting. She was divorced from Fairbanks by then, of course, but it was romantic anyway."

"Maybe romance lingers where it lived."

"Indeed it does." She smiled. "You're a sweet girl, Amelia; I'll miss you after graduation. They'll miss your help over at Bret Harte School for the Blind, too. I've heard some very good things about you from their principal. I understand you've been their best volunteer for two years now."

"Gee, I'm really interested in what you said about seeing Pickfair, Mrs. Watson. Is it still there?"

"I'm not certain, dear, I think it sustained some damage in the last big earthquake we had." She readjusted her glasses. "I do know that Mary Pickford refused to come out of the house in her later years. She wouldn't let anyone from the outside

6

take her picture either. I suppose she didn't want anyone to see her old."

I nodded. "She hid when she wasn't pretty anymore."

She sighed, shook her head, and looked at her watch. "Oh, snip snap! Less than five minutes to go. Time for me to gather my sheep." She blew her whistle and steered away some confused tourists who were trying to line up for our bus.

Shura breezed up. "Ah, what a relief!"

"You are so gross."

"I know it. I'm a good contrast to you, Little Miss Proper."

"Be quiet, or I'll hit you with my white gloves!"

"Come on! Let's go, they're leaving without us!" Shura grabbed my arm and dragged us toward the bus. "So, what's next on this fabulous field trip agenda?"

"The La Brea Tar Pits," I said.

"It's the pits, all right. How boring. It's just a big, stinky hole filled with black gunk and old dinosaur bones." She climbed onto the bus and headed to our seat. "Actually, it sounds just like my little brother's bedroom."

"At least after the pits, we get to go to the art museum."

"Art. That's more like it." She rubbed her hands together with glee, reached down into her backpack, and brought out her sketch pad and colored pencils. Shura could draw like a real artist.

"Are you going to sketch while we're there?"

"I'll try. But some of the guys think it's funny to run by and 'accidentally' bump into me. Some boys are such toads."

"I know. It's probably the same boys who bark at me and call me 'Fleabag.'"

"Ignore them. They bug everybody."

"That's what my mom says, too." I knew Mom and Shura were right, but some words are hard to shake off.

The bus turned onto Highland Avenue, headed for Sunset Boulevard, and we rumbled past the rolling green lawn of Hollywood Junior High. In the fall we'd all be going there; only three more weeks until graduation and the end of sixth grade.

The palm trees swayed as we drove by, and memories of another ending swayed into my mind's eye.

It was the last day of fifth grade, and I was all dressed up for the end of year certificate ceremony. Mom was there, with my little sister, Kate. Mom had on her nurse's uniform because she was on her lunch break; she checked her watch a lot.

Some of the boys made up a "class honors" list for the occasion. They printed it out on a home computer and distributed it as we filed out. I couldn't wait to get one and see what I had been voted.

My honor was "Most Likely to Never Get a Date."

I remember the look on Mom's face as she peered over my shoulder. I remember how the other kids laughed. I made myself laugh, too. Later, when I got home, I went to my room and stopped laughing.

After that, I wasn't a little kid anymore.

Now I looked out the bus window and caught my reflection. Amelia Fleeman—that nice, quiet, brown-haired girl who wears glasses and a furrowed brow. A teacher described me like that once and it sounded just about right to me.

"A ruble for your thoughts." Shura nudged me.

"Oh, nothing important," I lied.

"I just love the art museum," she mused. "Especially the Picasso stuff. It's so . . . unsettled."

"Yuk! Modern art bugs me! I like things to look the way they're supposed to. What I love is the Impressionist art, the stuff by Van Gogh, Manet, Monet, Renoir."

"What do you love about it?"

"One thing I like is that the women they painted weren't real skinny, like you have to be now and—"

"Who says you have to be?"

"—and also because of the way they used light and bright colors." I thought for a minute about the dream I had had the night before; everything in it was barren and brown. "I like the colors they used because my own life is kind of brown."

9

"Huh?"

"Well, you know. If *your* life was a color, Shura, it would be, I don't know, something rich and deep and royal. Like purple."

"Indubitably!"

"Mine would be flat and muted and quiet. You know, brown."

"Oh, come on, Amelia—"

"No, Shura. I'm right about this. My life is brown."

"There are different shades of brown, Amelia. It can be very pretty." She fanned her pencils in front of me.

"Nope. It's not a pretty color, at least not to me."

"But, Amelia . . ." Shura's strong voice grew a little less certain.

It didn't matter, I wasn't listening anymore. I turned to the window and imagined a different life for myself. "I'd like a light blue life," I said softly. My words settled on the window in a small, foggy cloud, then they evaporated.

"You guys got any gum?"

The request tumbled from the perfect, pink mouth of Wendy Lockwood, in the seat in front of us.

"*Nyet*," said Shura, not looking up. "Gum makes me resemble a large, cud-chewing cow. That's not my style."

Laughter tinkled over the seat. "Oh, Shura! You

really crack me up. Nobody can figure you out! Everyone thinks you're simply exotic."

"No, they don't. They think I'm weird. But it's no BFD to me."

Wendy shrugged and blinked her big, blue eyes in my direction. "Ah, Amanda, isn't it?"

"Amelia," I corrected patiently. People often got me wrong.

"Oh, yeah. Amelia, do you have any gum? Preferably sugarless?"

"No, sorry. I don't chew gum."

"Oh, no biggie. I'll get it from one of the boys. Thanks, anyway!" She smiled and wiggled her fingers at me and I noticed that her pale pink nail polish and lipstick matched exactly. Her curly, blond hair bounced around her shoulders when she turned away.

I sat in my brownness and gazed at her cover girl glow. I leaned my chin in my hand and bounced along with the rhythm of the bus wheels while pondering my favorite question: Why is life so lopsided?

2

I walked up the street toward our apartment complex. All the apartments on our street had been built in the 1960s and they each had a theme. I passed the Pirate's Cove and the Dolphin Splash. Here was ours: Tiki Village. I hated the six weird Hawaiian Tiki gods that stuck out of the grass near the entrance. One of them still leaned crazily sideways from the last earthquake.

The front door of our apartment stuck because of the heat, so I gave it a hard shove and tumbled into the room. My eight-year-old sister, Kate, was sitting on the floor playing both sides of a board game. "Who's winning?"

"Cyril is winning. He usually does. He is very intelligent, you know."

I went into the kitchen and got a diet soft drink.

"Hey, Kate, do you want to play with a real person? Because I don't mind playing with you for a little while."

"I *am* playing with a real person, Melia. I've told you and told you that Cyril plays with me." She laughed and moved her token. "Ha! I'll buy that and then I'll build hotels on it!"

I reached out and quickly waved my hand over the opposite side of the game board. "There's nobody there, Kate. Nada. Zip."

"He ducked." She eyed me and rolled the dice. "And he says for you to be more open-minded, or you'll never get a light blue life."

I practically gagged on the soda. "*What* did you say he said?"

"Come on, Melia, be quiet, I'm trying to win."

"What did Cyril say about me?" I stopped and took a quick mental inventory. Was I really asking my loony little sister what her imaginary friend had said?

"Something about the color of your life." She read the card in her hand and groaned. "Oh, no. I have to go straight to jail. I do not get to pass GO, I do not get two hundred dollars. Poopski."

"Don't change the subject. What did you mean about the color of my—oh, I get it. You heard me talking in my sleep last night. You're always telling me how I wake you up with my blabbing. I must have talked my way right through that brown dream."

"I don't know what you're blabbing about now. I told you what Cyril said."

"But he is *imaginary,* Kate. You make up what he says from what you hear. He can't really talk."

"He's only imaginary to you, 'cause you can't hear him," she said stubbornly.

"Well, this conversation is ridiculous, and besides, I have to start dinner. By the way, has Mom called?"

"No way, Jose. She's working an extra shift, remember? And what is LACMA, a secret club?"

"LACMA?"

"It's right there on your clothes."

"Oh, yeah." I removed the little pin. "That stands for Los Angeles County Museum of Art. My class went today for a field trip and they make you wear these little thingies to show that you're supposed to be there."

"Was it fun?"

"Yeah, it was really nice. If you come in the kitchen with me I'll tell you about it while I get dinner started."

"What are we having, and it better not have tofu in it."

"Stir-fry chicken," I yelled over the clatter of pans falling on top of each other.

"Okay, me and Cyril like Chinese food. Cyril

says cooking is an art, too. What art did you see today, Melia? Did they have those statues with no clothes on?" Kate came to stand near me.

"Yes, the naked statues were there, only it's called sculpture. There was impressionist art, modern art, and religious art. When we were all done, our teacher had the bus driver go by a real famous house, too."

"Pickfair?"

The slimy chicken breast slid out of my fingers and I stared at her. "Yeah, it was Pickfair. How'd you know about that?"

"Cyril just told me. Who's Mary Pickford, Cyril?"

"Come on, Kate, knock it off already. How'd you know?" Then I remembered the school books I had thrown on the couch. "Oh. You saw my folder where Shura did a sketch of Pickfair for me when we went by. I even wrote the name underneath, and who lived there. So that's really how you know, you saw it."

"I did not see it. Cyril *said* it." She stuck out her stubborn little jaw and chewed on one of her hair ribbons.

"Yeah, sure he did."

"You don't know anything, Amelia, and I don't want to keep you company anymore. Cyril and I have better things to do. Right, Cyril?"

* * *

Later that night after Kate was in bed, I thought I heard a noise from our room, so I put my book down and listened. It sounded as if people were talking and I felt my heart lurch. Oh, come on, I thought. Twelve and three quarters is too old to be acting so silly. I took two deep breaths and headed for the door. That's when I heard it again, but very clearly this time. A wispy voice said, "Amelia will be fine. Don't worry."

I held my breath and pushed the door open slowly. The night light cast an eerie glow. Kate muttered and wrestled with her sheets as she turned over. What a relief, I must have heard her talking in her sleep. We both do it all the time. There is always a logical explanation for weird stuff. But for a few minutes, I stood scared and silent at the edge of our room.

When I heard Mom's key in the door, I was so relieved, I ran over and hugged her.

"And here we have Fran Fleeman, world's most overworked, underpaid nurse!"

"What did I do to deserve this honor?"

"Can't I give my own mother a hug and a compliment?" She handed me her white sweater, and I hung it up.

"Oh, Amelia, I was just kidding." She gave me a funny look, but she smiled. "We *are* overworked, that's for sure. How I wish I could order new feet." Her white, clodhopper, nurses' shoes clattered to the floor as she put her feet up. "Boy, *Women in White* never looked like this."

"Life is never like those old movies, Mom. I made some dinner, you want some?"

"That would be great, I'm starved. And believe me, I know life isn't like those movies. I've learned it the hard way. But I wish it was, oh, how I wish."

I nuked a plate of food and handed it to her with a napkin. Then I plopped down next to her on the couch.

"Don't plop, dear." She set the plate on the coffee table. "Thanks a bunch." She removed her barrette from her thick, auburn hair and set it on the table. I stared at her hair and her big green eyes and wished we looked more alike.

"This looks good enough to eat, kiddo. Thanks for cooking again. I don't know what I'd do without you." She squeezed my hand. "I really appreciate the help. How was school?"

"Great."

A broccoli stalk dangled from her mouth. "Breally?"

"Yes, breally, but only because we went on a field trip."

"No wonder. You rarely define school as 'great.' "

"Well, today was different. We went to Mann's Chinese Theatre, the tar pits, and the museum. It was fun."

She nodded and chewed. "I'm happy to hear you

had fun. So what else happened? How was Katie's day? Did she remember her house key? I don't want her running around alone in the neighborhood; it just isn't safe anymore."

"She had her key around her neck. She was in here before me. Speaking of Katie, that reminds me, don't you think we should be worried about her and this imaginary Cyril of hers? She seems to be getting weirder and weirder about that guy, or ghost, or whatever the heck he is."

"I've talked to her about him, and it seems harmless enough to me. I don't think she drags him to school for show-and-tell, or anything."

"The 'show' part would be hard." I made a face. "She's almost nine now; isn't that a little old for an imaginary friend?"

"Technically, that's true. But, you know, Cyril joined us right after your father moved out. I always assumed it was her way of replacing him."

"I don't think I'd want to replace him."

"I know, I know. He was not a very happy camper, that's for sure. Hey, how about a cup of herbal tea before bed? Maybe we can even scrounge up a cookie or two."

"That would be good. Do we have some of that cranberry tea left?"

"Let's go take a peek!" She jumped up and I followed her. I watched her bustle around the kitchen as she told me about her day.

"Here you go, kiddo." She set a steaming mug in front of me and my glasses fogged up when I sniffed it.

We both giggled.

"Hmmm. Lots of mail," she said as she rifled through the stack. "But it's mostly bills, bills, and junk. I never get a letter." She munched on a Fig Newton.

"Nobody does, because nobody writes."

"Probably so. No child support, either."

"Why do you think he doesn't send it regularly?"

"He's probably out of work again. And he lives out of state, so it's hard to track him down."

"I'm kind of glad they can't track him down. I was always a little afraid he'd come back."

"I know. Sometimes I've even felt afraid, too. Being afraid is so crippling." She finished her tea. "But, the past is past. Time to move on."

I sat there and moved some Fig Newton crumbs around the table. The past isn't ever really past, I thought. You carry it around forever. The line of a poem we read in English popped into my head: "I am a part of all that I have met."

I undressed quietly by the dim glow of the night light.

"Is Mommy home okay?" Kate's sleepy voice found me in the semi-darkness.

"Yes, she's fine. Don't worry. Hey, don't forget,

tomorrow is Friday and a teacher workday, so we can go downtown and try to get some free tickets to the TV shows."

"Can we go to the Candy K. Crowley show? I don't want to go to anymore game shows. People scream too much at those."

"We'll have to see. Whatever they're handing out on Hollywood Boulevard is where we can go. I'm not sure if Candy tapes her talk show in town this week, or if she's on the road right now."

"Cyril says she's here in Hollywood." She yawned. "Move over, Cyril, you're right on the edge of the bed. It's squishy."

I instinctively pulled my nightgown over my chest. Or at least, where my chest would be, if I had one. "Tell him not to peek, okay?"

"He's not like people, Melia. He doesn't care what you look like on the outside."

"Where is he?" I picked out my clothes for the next day and put them on the chair. My California summer uniform: shorts, tee shirt, and flip-flops.

"He's usually behind me to the left. Unless he's playing a game with me." She flipped her pillow over to the cool side. "Boy, it's hot, and it isn't even June. I feel like a hot dog on a cooker."

I turned off the night light and climbed into bed. "I guess it's nice to have an imaginary friend, huh? I mean, there aren't any kids your age around here. You spend a lot of time alone, or with me."

20

"That's not why I have him and he's not imagi-nary."

"Then what is he?"

"Cyril says there is no such thing as imaginary friends, there—"

"Oh boy! So you finally admit that he's made up and he agrees with you." This was an interesting turn of strange events.

"No, silly, you didn't let me finish. There are no imaginary friends, there are only guardian an-gels."

"Okay, then do I have one?"

"Yep."

"Where is it?"

"Right there, always by you."

"Why can't I see it?"

"Don't ask me."

"You seem like the perfect choice."

"Cyril says if you ask your angel, you'll always get an answer."

"I don't think so."

She turned over. "I tried, Cyril. I tried."

3

Kate and I took the bus downtown the next day and strolled along Hollywood Boulevard; we called it Hollyweird, though.

The regular crazies were roaming around. Harold, the balloon man, was on the corner. He wore balloon hats and balloon jewelry. He said he lived in a balloon.

Aggie, the cat lady, was on her regular bus stop bench. She had four cats which she kept on little leashes; they went everywhere with her. Which wasn't very far, because she always seemed to be in the same spot.

The Bean Can Man was there. He saved all the cans he ate from and dragged them around with him. They made quite a clatter when he went by.

Mom was always warning me to be careful on

the Boulevard. But these people weren't scary or mean. They just seemed to be on a different wavelength.

Kate and I headed straight for the Hollywood Walk of Fame. That's where famous people get a star put right into the sidewalk with their name on it. I liked to dream about my own name being there: Amelia Fleeman, actress. Maybe I should change Fleeman, though. Amelia Martin sounded better. I figured I could be a character actress and play all the roles the other actresses were too pretty for.

"How come Mickey Mouse has a star, but not Goofy or Donald Duck? They're famous too." Kate tugged on my hand.

"I don't know. I guess they're not famous enough." My eyes glazed over as I imagined receiving my own star on the Walk of Fame.

Kate yanked me back to reality. "Melia, here comes one of those free ticket guys. Let's see if he has Candy Crowley."

The studios send their people out with tickets to all sorts of shows. It's free to get into all tapings of sitcoms, talk shows, and game shows. So they have guys running around Hollywood looking for tourists and local people to help fill up the audience.

"Hey, mister?" Katie pulled on the sleeve of the ticket man.

"What can I do for you, cutie?"

I waited. I knew he wasn't done yet.

"You are as cute as a button, aren't you? Where'd you get those freckles and that pretty red hair?"

I sighed. I wasn't jealous of Katie's much-commented-on cuteness, just envious.

Okay, maybe jealous every other time.

"I got 'em from my mom," answered Kate. "Can me and my sister see the Candy K. Crowley show today? Please?"

"Let me see here . . ." He rifled through his stack. "You bet. She's real popular, you know." He handed me the tickets. "You better get over to CBS Television Center as soon as you can. You'll need to get in line pretty quick, if you want to get a good seat."

"Um, sir?"

He looked at me over his shades.

"Which bus do we take over there?"

"You take the one that says Farmer's Market on it. I think it's the Eighty-nine. That will put you right next to CBS."

"Thanks very much," I called as he walked away.

He was right. The line was long, but not too long for us. Kate and I watched the Candy Crowley show nearly every afternoon after school. Candy had, absolutely, the very best talk show of anyone. It was interesting, but not stupid. We'd been talking about going to see a taping for months.

"I wonder what the subject is today?" Katie wondered aloud.

The woman in front of us turned around. She was square-shaped and wore purple spandex shorts, an orange tank top, and had dyed red hair. Her glasses hung around her neck on a pearly, plastic chain. "I hope she does something unusual," she confided, blowing cigarette smoke out the side of her mouth. "Like people who have ESP or something."

"Or how about the shows where whole families get on there and talk about their personal problems. I can't believe people do that!" I said as I tried to avoid breathing in the smoke screen she was creating.

The lady laughed. There was orange lipstick smeared on her front tooth. I wondered if all older ladies had lipstick smeared permanently on their teeth. I tried to stop staring at her mouth as she spoke.

"I guess most of us would do or say just about anything to get on the television," she said lipstickily. "I know I would!" She ground out her cigarette with the toe of her Egyptian sandal.

We were broiling under the California sun, so I ran over to the Farmer's Market and bought cold drinks for me, Katie, and the orange lipstick lady.

Everyone in the line cheered when they finally let us inside at three o'clock. They put us through a metal detector before we could go in the studio. "In case of guns," I whispered to Kate.

Next they checked our bags for cameras. "No photographs allowed!" barked the guard.

Finally, we were led into the studio, where a giant red kiss imprint puckered at us from the wall. That was Candy's trademark. Her commercials always said the *K* in her name stood for Kiss.

Some man came out for the warm-up. That's the part you can't see at home, where they tell jokes just to the audience so everyone will be in a fun mood. Then they show the applause sign and pretty much command you to laugh and clap when you see it go on. He made us practice. At four o'clock, the music swelled, the lights went down and the announcer yelled, "Ladies and gentlemen, give a warm greeting to our own, Candy Kiss!"

We cheered and clapped and stomped. Some guys in the back yelled "Woop, woop, woop!" I looked over at Katie. She was trying to whistle by using her fingers. Mostly she was just spitting, though.

Candy came out and waved and smiled and sat on her special chair. She was wearing a bright pink jump suit with a big turquoise belt. I admired her; she had her own style.

"Hi, everyone! I'm very happy to see all of you here in our studio audience, and I send a big kiss to those of you watching at home!" She threw a big kiss toward the camera. "Today, we have a truly wonderful show. And I mean, full of wonder!"

Kate and I looked at each other and shrugged.

"I'm particularly entranced by today's subject. It's something I've wondered about for a long time, and lately, I've noticed that the rest of the country is just as fascinated as I am. After this message, we'll come back to discuss guardian angels. Are they real, imaginary, or just wishful thinking?"

I nearly fell off my chair.

4

"**W**asn't that just the greatest show? All those *grown-ups* with guardian angels! I bet now you believe in them, don't you?" Kate crossed her arms and beamed at me from her perch on the bus stop bench.

"Not necessarily." I fished around in my purse for our bus passes. "Those people could have made up all those stories about angels."

"I think *you're* crazy not to believe in angels."

"No, crazy is that one lady on the show who talked about how nothing is a coincidence."

"I didn't get that part."

"You know, the lady who had all the jangly jewelry on. She said every single thing that happens, has a special reason. I mean, come on, some things are just a fluke."

28

Just then, out of the corner of my always-wary eye, I saw two teenaged boys swagger up to our stop. I put my guard up, and turned, like a shield, toward Kate.

They came around in front of us.

"Hey, four eyes, which bus is comin' next?" asked the taller one.

I shrugged.

He poked his smaller friend. "Hey, that's cool. She's ugly *and* stupid."

I stared straight ahead, not blinking, and barely breathing. I prayed that the approaching bus was theirs. It wheezed to a stop and opened its doors; they clambered on.

If things happen for a reason, then what was that for? I asked silently.

"Your nails sure do look good today," Kate said softly.

"Thanks, sis." I looked down at my best feature—my long, tapered hands, and strong nails.

Kate pulled her legs up and leaned her chin on her boney little knees. "Hey, Melia, did you fill out the suggestion card they gave you at the end of the Candy K. Crowley show? What did you put? I put that I think they should have a show about famous animals. Like, they could have Lassie, and Rin Tin Tin, and the cat from that Disney movie, and that monkey from the TV show. They could show us how they get them to do all that neat stuff."

"Sounds good."

"Did you do a card, Amelia?"

I looked at the billboard over our heads. A beautiful, big-chested, blond girl, holding an icy glass of something smiled down at me. "Yep. I said I thought they should do a show about girls who aren't very pretty. Not a make-over show either, where they load gobs of stuff on your face. Just a show about how we, or they, feel. What it's like to be plain in a pretty world."

"You're not plain. I think you're real pretty, so does Mommy, and so does Cyril."

Quite a cheering section. A mother, a sister, and an invisible man. I nodded at Kate and stared at the traffic.

"Oh, hey there, Andrea!" Wendy Lockwood smiled at me from the bright red '64 Mustang convertible idling in front of us.

"It's Amelia. And this is my little sister, Kate."

"Dad, can't we please give them a ride? It's so hot out. They look all melty."

"Well, I suppose so." Mr. Lockwood looked at us over the top of his sunglasses. "Go ahead and get in girls, but please be sure your feet are clean."

Remembering our apartment complex with those stunning Tiki heads in our working class neighborhood, I started to say no thanks. Too late. Katie was already in the back seat, bouncing up and down on the creamy, white leather.

"Come on, Melia! Get in!"

I paused on the edge of the curb. Wendy and her father seemed to shimmer with perfection in the sun. It was like climbing into a commercial. Attractive, but not quite real.

"Thank you very much, Mr. Lockwood." I poked Kate. "Stop bouncing around," I whispered.

"Where do you live?" asked Mr. Lockwood.

I gave the directions.

"Oh," he said. "I'm not too familiar with that part of town."

We drove along in silence. Mr. Lockwood pointed at the CD player. "Put in a new disc, Wendy. And be careful to do it correctly. Don't touch the surface."

"Okay, Daddy. Which one?"

"Well, what do you want to hear?"

"Oh, I think I like, um, maybe soft rock music?"

He made a face.

"But, I also like classical music, just like you. How about the Four Seasons?"

"Perhaps you should ask your friends what they like to hear. Remember your manners." He tapped impatiently on the steering wheel when the light changed to red.

"What kind of music do you guys want?"

I shrugged noncommittally.

"*Wow!* Who cares what music you play?" squealed Kate. "I can't believe you have that in your car. We only have two clock radios and a record player in our whole house!"

Great! She made us sound like the Beverly Hillbillies! I nudged her and shook my head, but she prattled on.

"You must be, like the richest people in the whole town!"

"You are such a cutie!" said Wendy. "How about some classical music? That's really what my dad likes best, right, Daddy?"

"I believe we've established that, Wendy."

Mr. Lockwood was handsome, tall and tan. He wore white shorts and an open-necked, navy blue sport shirt with a little polo player embroidered over the pocket. I saw him look at me in the rear-view mirror, but because of his sunglasses, I couldn't see his eyes. It reminded me of the kids at the school for the blind where I volunteer. A lot of them wear sunglasses, too. But for a different reason.

Kate took a pack of gum out of her pink Elvis Presley purse. "Anybody want some of my bubble gum?"

"Put that away!" ordered Mr. Lockwood.

"Sorry." She made herself small.

"We don't eat in our car, it's against the rules," explained Wendy quietly.

"That's right," Mr. Lockwood said. "A car is not an appropriate place to eat."

I looked at Katie and we sat back. Carefully and quietly.

The convertible glided up to our apartment complex. The Tiki gods leered at me.

Wendy got some paper out of her purse. "Listen, I guess I forgot to tell you. Daddy is letting me have a catered swim party at my house tomorrow night." She glanced quickly at him. "It'll be a real quiet, nice party. Kind of an almost-end-of-school bash. Why don't you come? And be sure to bring Shura, she's your best friend, right?"

"Yes, I'm friends with Shura."

Mr. Lockwood cleared his throat. "Wendy, will you watch that pen on this leather upholstery?"

"Oh, sorry, Daddy." She finished writing the time and the directions using her leg as support. "I hope you can come. It'll be a lot of fun!"

As they pulled away I noticed the license plate. It read 1 4 WAYNE.

"Are you going? Are you going? I'd go!" Kate stopped to rub one of the Tiki tummies. She insisted it gave her good luck.

She hopped after me up to our door. "I'd go just to see their house. I bet it's filled with big screen TVs, VCRs, cordless phones, and CD players!"

I ignored her, or tried to, while I thought about the invitation and jiggled the key in the old lock.

"I'd sure like to go to their house. It's probly the

kind of house you only see on TV shows. Her dad doesn't seem like a TV dad, though."

"Well, I can kind of see it, Katie." I closed and locked the door. "I mean, restoring that car probably cost a zillion dollars. He wants to keep it nice. And CDs are expensive, too."

"I guess. Hey, looky, there's a note from Mommy on the table." She hopped over and picked it up. "It says, 'Dear girls, I went grocery shopping. Back in a bit. Don't eat all the See's chocolates, they were a gift from one of my patients. Love, Mom.'"

Kate raised the lid off the box and sniffed the chocolatey fumes. "Yeah, Cyril. I think See's is the nectar of the gods, too." She selected a candy from its paper nest, flipped it over and poked her little pinkie into it.

"Hey!" I yelped, and lunged for her. "Don't do that! Mom hates it when you poke them! She'll kill *me* if you do it."

"That's why I do it! How am I supposed to know which one I like, if I don't poke at it?" She rejected the one in her hand and poked another one.

"You have to eat that one now," I said with mock authority. "Whatever it is!"

"No way, Jose. It's coconut! I hate that! It's like white grass!"

"Chew it up!" I tried to fit the candy between her lips.

She laughed and clamped her jaw tight, but I

34

managed to wedge it in through a laugh crack.

"Okay, now you've got to eat the other one you poked."

"*Nooo!* Irt's gukky, with chleery in it!"

I wedged the chleery one in, too. "There! That's what you get!"

"That's what *you* get!" she wheezed merrily and pointed at her feet.

"Oh, yukko! I can't believe it! You spit chocolate all over the kitchen floor!" I laughed and clutched my stomach as tears rolled down my face. "We have to hurry and clean it up! Before Mom comes home!"

Kate couldn't hurry to do anything. Her mouth hung open in a long, silent, chocolate laugh.

That started me laughing all over again. And that's how Mom found us; laughing hysterically in a pool of chewed chocolate. She just shook her head and handed us a roll of paper towels.

"And when you've finished with the floor, start on yourselves!" she pointed at the bathroom door.

After we cleaned up the mess, and ourselves, we told Mom all about the Candy K. Crowley show over dinner.

"And afterward, at the bus, we got a ride from a girl in Amelia's class." Kate drank her milk and admired her foamy, white moustache in the bowl of her spoon.

"Amelia, you shouldn't accept rides from people you don't know well. You know it's not safe." Mom gave me her "you're the oldest" look.

"Come on, Mom." I raised my fork in defense. "You know I wouldn't hitchhike or take rides from people I don't know. This was Wendy Lockwood and her dad was driving. You've heard of him, haven't you? He's some famous divorce lawyer to the stars."

"Oh. You mean Wayne L. Lockwood? He was recently in the *L.A. Times* in that article about art collectors, wasn't he?"

"Uh-huh. I think Shura mentioned something about that story to me."

"Me and Cyril were amazed, Mommy." Kate leaned forward and put her elbows in her salad. "They had so much stuff in their car! They could practically live in it, I bet!"

"You should have seen her, Mom. She was bouncing around in the back seat of their convertible, like little Miss Muffet on her tuffet—"

"Cyril," Kate interrupted, "would like to remind you that it's rude to discuss people whether they are invisible, or not." She rolled up her napkin and stuck it out from her forehead. "I'm a unicorn," she pronounced. Then she rammed me with her horn. I laughed, so she smiled contentedly and turned back to Mom. "Know what else happened? The girl

36

in the car, Wendy, she invited Melia to a swim party!"

"Geez, I completely forgot! She asked me and Shura to a party at her house tomorrow. Can I go?"

"May I, and yes, I guess it would be okay. I'm off tomorrow night."

"Great! I've got to call Shura right now!" I jumped up—rattling the table and Mom's nerves.

"Hello, dear. Yes, I vill get her," said Mrs. Najinsky.

As soon as I heard Shura pick up, I babbled the whole story.

"I'm not going," she said. "No way on earth would you get me up there to that house of snobs on the hill."

"Remember, they have that famous art collection."

"BFD."

"Listen, Shura. Mr. Lockwood might be a snob on a hill, and he might not be. But he likes art, and according to you, that means he can't be all bad, now can he?"

"Wellllll . . ."

The fish was interested. I almost had my catch. I jiggled the line, just a bit.

"Come on, Shura. I'd be too chicken to go alone."

I waited for her answer and thought about the Candy Crowley show. If nothing is a coincidence, then maybe I was meant to go to this party! Even if it did mean appearing in public in my dreaded bathing suit.

"Do I have to swim at this swim party? You know I never learned to swim. I refuse to become a sun-drenched, water-logged, leathery Californian."

"No, Shura. They won't *make* you swim. Just come because I want you to."

"All right, all ready! I suppose it won't kill me. Maybe I'll even get a glimpse of the art. He's supposed to have some pretty famous stuff up there."

"Great! We'll pick you up around seven."

"Okay. See you then."

"Ah, Shura?"

"Yeah?"

"Do you believe in guardian angels?"

"What?"

"Guardian angels. I saw a show about them today, and I just wondered . . ."

"No, not really." The line went silent for a moment. "But, you know, now that you mention it, I did have an imaginary friend once. When I was a little girl she came over with me from Russia."

"What happened to her?"

"I don't remember exactly. I guess she disappeared when I stopped believing in her."

5

"**W**ow! Look at that view!" Mom carefully maneuvered our old, yellow Volkswagen Beetle up the winding road that led to the land of the Lockwoods.

"Pretty spiffy. I bet you can even see the HOLLYWOOD sign from the Lockwood's house," said Shura.

"Did you know that the sign used to blink off and on with five thousand lights, and say HOLLYWOOD-LAND? And Peg Entwistle, a young starlet from England, killed herself by jumping off the fifty-foot high letter *H* back in the 1930s," I informed my captive audience, as I craned my neck for a better view.

"That's a cheery tale. Thanks for sharing it," said Mom.

"It's awful, but it's true! She came here to be a

star, and they cancelled her contract after only one movie. She was crushed."

"Especially when she landed," deadpanned Shura.

"Yuk." I made a face at her.

She ignored me and rearranged her caftan. "That's what happens when you buy the line they feed you around here."

"What line is that, dear?" asked Mom.

"The line that if you're not astonishingly beautiful, then your whole life is useless and you should go live under a rock or throw yourself off a giant letter."

"That's right, there are more important things than looks and money," Mom said.

"Personally, I think you're both nuts." I picked some lint off the flowered sundress I had painstakingly chosen to wear. "I'd love to be pretty. So pretty that people stop on the street and stare at me, with their mouths hanging open. In fact, I wouldn't mind looking like Marilyn Monroe."

"And we all know what happened to her," said Shura.

"I said I wanted to look like her, not die like her," I retorted. "It would be nice to be pretty and have whatever I want."

"And then what?" asked Shura.

"What do you mean?"

40

"What would you do? Sit around and be rich and pretty? Stare at yourself all day? Frantically watch for wrinkles? Shop all day? You hate to shop. I've experienced *that* firsthand!"

"No, it just seems as if I hate to shop because I hate how I look in the mirrors in all those dressing rooms."

Shura rolled her eyes. "It's no use talking to you! You've been brainwashed."

"That's right, Amelia. You are a lovely girl, with a warm personality. If you were so awful, would you have been invited to this nice party?" asked Mom, being maternal. And, I suspected, hopeful.

"Oh, Mom, wake up and smell the smog! I know Wendy only invited me because I'm Shura's friend, and she wants Shura to come because she thinks she's so strange and exotic."

"It's true, I am a rare bird." She yanked on her caftan. "Get off my plumage, will you?"

We pulled through a gate guarded by snarling, stone lions and then into a long, circular driveway.

"We're here!" said Mom. "You know, this looks just like the house in *The Philadelphia Story* with Cary Grant and Katharine Hepburn. Maybe they shot it here back in the 1930s."

"Maybe." I sighed. "Just look at this place, it is so huge! And so beautiful! Look at those flowers lining the walk, they are so perfect, they almost look plastic."

"Let's get in there to perfect, plastic land before I change my mind." Shura got out and surveyed the house skeptically. "BFD," she muttered.

"Have a wonderful time girls, and call me when it's over!" said Mom. Then she chugged back down the hill.

"Look at it," I whispered. "Can you imagine living here? Look at the lawn; it looks manicured. Those gardens look as if a weed wouldn't dare grow in them."

"Yeah, yeah, it's perfectly perfect. Let's get in there and get this over with." She pulled me toward the door and rang the bell.

A maid opened it.

I nearly fell off the porch. I'd only seen maids in old movies.

"Good evening, girls," she said with a thick accent. "Please, you come this way to back terrace."

The backyard was breathtaking. Chinese lanterns swayed in the breeze, casting a colorful glow over the pool, which was shaped like a giant kidney bean. There was a diving board buried in a rock garden at the far end. Near the house was a large, bricked patio with a huge barbecue, built right in. The view from up here was spectacular!

Los Angeles glittered in the distance; a well-advertised mirage.

"It looks as if almost the whole sixth grade class is here," said Shura as she scanned. "Even all the outsiders and renegades. The only ones missing are the druggies."

"I don't care who is missing. I'm just so glad to be invited."

"This isn't the White House, Amelia. These are just rich people. BFD."

"Well, it's a BFD to me!"

She laughed and shook her head. "Okay."

"Hi, you guys!" Wendy bounced up to us. She wore a pale pink, strapless sundress, with a single strand of pearls. Her hair was piled on her head, with teeny pink and white flowers entwined. Her straight, white teeth showed between pretty, pink lips. Her always zit-free face glowed.

I felt the flowers on my dress fade.

"Shura, I can't believe you came! You never go to anybody's party; it's so cool that you picked mine to come to!"

"I only came because Amelia said that you told her that if—"

I stomped on Shura's sandal and shook my head.

"Come on, let me show you around!" Wendy tried to lead Shura away.

"No, that's okay. I'll just hang here for a while and admire the view."

"Oh, okay. I'll be back to check on you as soon as everybody has arrived!" Wendy flitted off to greet some freshly-awed arrivals.

"Don't tell her I made you come," I whispered. "You might make her feel bad. Try and be a good little Shura, will you?"

"Come on, she only invited me because she hopes I'll do something weird."

"And she only invited me, to get to you! So be nice."

"That's *not* why she invited you. You're not Quasimodo, Amelia. People like you just fine, you always back off before they have a chance to—Hey! Look over there—a whole table full of Chinese food. Let's go!"

"Wait, Shur. Isn't that Bill Thomas in line at that buffet table?"

"So?"

"So! You know darned well I've had a crush on him since third grade. I don't want to get in line right behind him!"

"Why not? You don't smell, do you?"

"Ha, ha. I couldn't smell, I took two showers before I came and I'm wearing just the right amount of perfume."

"Then what's wrong?"

"I'm sure that I'll say some moronic thing if he speaks to me, not that he's likely to, but he might. He is so drop-dead gorgeous, I get all lost in his

44

eyes, or his smile, or something. In fifth grade they made us square dance and he was my partner for a whole week. It was heaven, except he kept calling me Cornelia."

"Spare me the gory details, will you? You're going to ruin my appetite."

"Let's just wait till some more people go over there, okay?"

"Calm down, Amelia. There go Rosalinda Rodriguez and Whitney Cox to coo and gurgle over him and keep him occupied. Now can we go eat?"

"Okay."

We piled our plates with egg rolls, fried rice, and sweet-and-sour pork. At least, Shura did. I didn't want to scarf down too many calories, and then have my stomach stick out like an inflated balloon.

People from the catering company came out regularly and refilled the dishes. They even had waiters come around with fresh drinks on little trays, and there was nothing from a can, either!

The smell of chlorine and Chinese food mingled in the air, and party music wafted over us. Some of the kids were dancing on the patio.

"I wish somebody would ask me to dance," I said, dreamily.

"Do you know how?" Shura wiped sweet-and-sour sauce from her fingers.

"Sort of. I practice at home sometimes with that dance show on TV."

"It's probably different with a live specimen wriggling around in front of you."

"Especially if Bill was the wriggler." I swayed in my seat. "I've imagined him asking me to dance or go out on a date."

"I bet that's not all you've imagined," she said wickedly.

The flush crept around my whole head. "Shush, Shura."

"Okay. Listen, I'm going inside to look for the famous art collection. You coming?"

"No. If I perch here long enough, maybe I'll work up the courage to go in the pool. But I'll probably just sit and watch everybody else."

"Sounds enthralling. But maybe wishes do come true up here on the hill, right?"

"You never know, maybe someone *will* ask me to dance."

"If he does, make him get your name right!" She swept off into the house.

I hummed to the music and tried to see if Bill was still dancing, and if so, who the lucky girl was. I jumped when someone came up behind me and touched my arm.

"Hey, ahhh, we're trying to get enough people together for a big game of Marco Polo. Do you want to play?"

I looked up into the long-lashed, brown eyes of Bill Thomas.

"Um, well, I don't know. I told Shura I'd wait here for her . . ."

"Come on! It's really fun! I'll even be 'it'!"

"I'm not sure . . ."

"Okay, well, when you are, just jump in! The more who play, the better the game!" He grinned and went around to gather some other kids.

I sat there and waited for my heart to go back to normal. What a witty response, I silently chided myself. Of course, he didn't really want *me*, he was asking everyone.

According to my watch, Shura had been gone for over half an hour. I supposed I should get up and mingle or something, but I didn't have a clue how to do that. There were regular articles in *Seventeen* about being popular at parties, but none of the advice seemed to apply to girls like me. It's tough to be warm and witty when you're wary.

"Hey, Amelia, enjoying the party, I see."

I jumped. It was just Richard Flink. He'd been alphabetized into my life ever since third grade. I probably had permanent pencil pokes in my back where he'd nailed me over the years.

"Hi, Richard. Yes, it's very nice, isn't it?"

"I was being facetious. You look pretty miserable. But that's how these events are for us outcasts. They invite us just to exclude us."

"We are not us, Richard. I'm sorry if you feel excluded, but I don't. I'm having a nice time and I don't feel excluded at all. I want to watch. I like watching."

"You said you don't feel excluded twice. 'The lady doth protest too much, methinks.' "

"Richard, you're the only person I know who quotes Shakespeare."

"Yeah, me and the Bard are buds. I not only quote him, I read him!" He took off his glasses and wiped them with his shirt. "The fact that both my parents are Lit professors might have something to do with that little quirk. My mother says she read the plays out loud while she gave me my bottle."

I nodded absently and tried to spot Bill in the water.

"So, are you going to swim, or don't you want to unveil the old swimsuit number? Personally, I'm keeping my shirt on. Too skinny for my own good. Heh, heh."

Richard had the annoying habit of reading my mind.

"Silence speaks volumes, I always say," he continued. "Not that anyone listens to me." He grinned and his top lip got caught in the grillwork of his braces. "You can't fool me. You fit in here like a pickle dipped in chocolate. Face it, you're like

48

me: on the outside lookin' in. In fact, our noses are permanently squashed from being pressed up against the glass."

"See you later, Richard. I need to go find Shura." I brushed his remarks away and headed for the house.

The house was just as pretty on the inside as on the outside. Everything was color coordinated, right down to the phones and the tissue boxes! The carpet was pale and thick, and it quieted my footsteps. It was a house you would see in a magazine about houses. I tried to imagine how different my life would be if it were lived in a house like this!

I wandered down a hallway that was covered with family photos and paused at a picture of a thin, blond woman who was holding Wendy. I stared into the woman's big, anxious eyes. She looked like a frightened fawn, caught in a sudden beam of headlights.

"Pardon me, young lady, but the house isn't open for tours."

I turned with a start.

"The party is outside." Mr. Lockwood crossed his arms and pursed his lips.

"Sorry, Mr. Lockwood. I guess I took a wrong turn, I'm just looking for someone."

"Look elsewhere." He strode away, and I heard a door slam.

The knickknacks on a corner shelf rattled dangerously.

6

"**O**h, there you are!" said Shura. "I've been look-ing all over this maniac mansion for you! I finally decided to sit in one spot until you reappeared." She scooted over on her deck chair to make room for me.

"I've been looking for you, too."

"You were? Did you hear what happened to me?"

"No."

"Mr. Lockwood found me in the east wing library gazing at his precious art and he had a conniption fit. I asked the maid first, if it was okay, and she said it was. Wouldn't you think he'd want to have people appreciate the stuff? I could *not* believe it! He was ranting and raving at the top of his lungs. I'd hate to live in this fancy cage. Hey, are you listening to me? What's wrong with you? You look as if you're not quite present and accounted for."

"Nothing's wrong." I dragged my eyes away from Bill, who was laughing and dunking girls in the water. They squealed and clung to him like little love barnacles. "I'm listening to you, Shur."

"Coulda' fooled me. Why don't you go in the pool? I know they were draggin' the place trying to get people to play that dumb game. You wore your suit. Why don't you go ahead and get in! Get your feet wet, take the plunge."

"No, I don't want to go in. I'm just fine right here with you. So tell me, what exactly happened with you and Mr. Lockwood?"

"Believe me, you don't want to know exactly what he said. Just be thankful you don't have to live here. That guy is just a big bully in an expensive suit."

"Listen up, everyone!" Wendy appeared at the sliding glass doors to the patio. She wore the scoop-necked, high-thigh bathing suit that was featured in the latest issue of *Seventeen*. She filled it up in all the right places. "My dad says it's time to wind this up, so you all need to get dried off and call home. You can use the pool house if you need a changing room, and there are fresh towels in there, too."

"This little heave-ho announcement is probably thanks to me," whispered Shura. "He wants the riffraff out of the palace."

"Also," continued Wendy, "since I'm class secretary, I need anyone who is going to the graduation dance to *please* sign up. The list is near the telephone. The principal said we need to know *now* so we can plan for refreshments. Don't forget, we're having a live band, too!"

"They're sure making a big deal out of that dance," I grumbled. "It's been announced everyday, it's on posters all over the halls, and it was in the PTA newsletter. It'll probably be on a TV commercial next! They advertise it like it's a trip to Paris, or something."

"It would be a trip to Paree, if the lucky girl went with me!"

I turned. "Oh, hi, Richard. Nice rhyme."

"Try to contain your enthusiasm at my sudden, poetic appearance, Fleeman. You wouldn't want me to get the wrong idea, or anything. Hey, Najinsky, how ya doin'?"

"Fine, Flinky, just fine."

"*Are* you two going to the dance?" he asked.

"Not me," said Shura. "My parents are dragging me off to Russia to visit the old homeland, practically as soon as they hand us our diplomas. The land of my people calls to me, only I can hardly understand what it's saying anymore."

He looked expectantly at me. "What about the quiet Fleeman? Prince Charming call yet?"

"Nobody's asked me."

"Well," he swallowed and his Adam's apple jumped. "I sort of meant—"

"Hey, what's cookin' over here in the corner? You guys better get in line for the phone, or you'll end up sleeping here on the deck chairs, and my dad would not be pleased!" Wendy smiled anxiously and directed us inside to the phone.

We were all hanging around out front, waiting for our rides. I watched Bill as he messed around with the other guys. He looked so cute, all damp and disheveled and devilish. It was weird how I was so aware of him—every move, every gesture—and he barely knew I was alive.

Something caught my eye. Richard Flink was leaning against the house. He gave me the boy scout salute. I nodded.

"Ameeeelia!" said Shura. "What is it with you tonight? Every time I talk to you, I have to drag you back from whatever planet you're visiting." She waved her hand in front of my face. "Earth to Amelia. Please leave your answering machine on."

"Sorry. I was thinking about the graduation dance . . . and stuff."

"You really want to go to that thing, don't you?"

I nodded. "I've never been to a big dance like this; I went to an after-school dance once and hid in a corner the whole time. This is our first fancy dance, the kind where you get a date, dress up, and go somewhere nicer than the gymnasium."

"If you really want to go, I think Flinky was try-ing to ask you back there."

"No. He was just fooling around. He's always teasing me. If I did say yes, he'd probably just laugh and make a joke out of it. We're really just school friends."

"You could ask a guy you like to go with you. That's what I'd do, if I really wanted to go. I think boys get nervous and they need a nudge. So I'd nudge 'em."

"I'm not you, Shura."

"That's good." She peeked inside her caftan. "It'd be pretty crowded in here."

Wendy tapped Shura on the shoulder. "I heard my dad got upset with you earlier. I'm really sorry if it bothered you."

"No bother."

"He's not so bad, really. You just have to handle him the right way. I'd like you to come over again, but you'll need to apologize to my dad first. Okay?"

"No way. I didn't do anything—"

"Listen for a minute." Wendy lowered her voice. "You just need to be quiet, like a little mouse, and do what he says. Then say you're sorry. He even buys me a present after he gets real mad." She fingered the pearls around her neck. "He's not so bad."

"Thanks, but no thanks," said Shura.

Wendy shrugged and walked away.

"The trouble with being like a mouse," whispered Shura, "is that you might get the cheese, but the trap hurts like hell."

I smiled. "Come on, you Russian wonder woman, here's Mom in the vee dub, let's go."

Wendy and the other kids called good-bye and waved.

"I feel like the queen," Shura said regally as she waved from the front window. "Good-bye, my subjects! Be well!"

And I'm the lady-in-waiting, I thought as we drove away.

"So? How was it, girls? Did you have a good time?"

"Depends on how you define good. I think maybe interesting, is more like it," said Shura.

Mom stopped at a light and looked back at me. "You're awfully quiet, kiddo. Was it interesting to you, too?"

"It was pretty nice, Mom. I just don't know if I fit in there or not. I felt like a fish out of water."

"Literally," cracked Shura.

"Why wouldn't you fit in?" asked Mom.

"I don't know. I just think they all know the right thing to say and do, and I don't."

"Hah!" said Shura. "The joke is that nobody knows and they're all afraid it will show!"

* * *

"Come on, let's watch an old movie on cable," said Mom when we got home. "Come and sit by me."

"Which one?" I kicked off my shoes and curled up next to her.

"*Sabrina* is on. It stars Audrey Hepburn as the daughter of a chauffeur, and two rich brothers fall in love with her. Then she has to choose between them."

"Oh, so it's a fantasy."

"Har, har. You certainly are my practical one, aren't you?"

"I think I'm just realistic."

"Just let yourself get swept up in the romance."

"I'll try."

I ended up falling asleep on the couch.

"Wake up, kiddo, time to go to bed," whispered Mom as she brushed the hair out of my eyes. "You fell asleep."

"Oh, sorry, Mom."

"That's okay. I forgot to tell you, there was a phone call for you earlier when you were at the party. I was soaking in the tub, so I didn't take the message. Katie took it, and it's kind of garbled. She taped it to the bathroom mirror."

"I'll go see." I sat up, stretched and yawned. "So, what happened at the end? Which brother did Audrey marry?"

"The one she loved, of course."

"I know, but which—"

"I'm not telling! You might want to watch this movie again someday when you're older and have fallen in love."

"How do you know I haven't?"

I left her sitting there, mouth hanging open.

The bathroom light flickered on and my eyes focused on the note that was stuck to my mirror-chin.

Melia. Some laydee called for you. She said she call bak later. She wants to talk to you about girls who are plane. I luv you. Katie, your sis, and Cyril is here to. P.S. Did you hav fun up ther at the party on the hill?

I smiled. She should let Cyril take the messages, I thought. Probably somebody selling beauty cream, and they heard I could use some. Hey, maybe it's Mary Pickford Beauty Cream; rub it on, and you never grow old! I sighed. What must it have been like for her? Locked up in that big house, trying to avoid her own face.

I looked at mine in the mirror. I put on some Acne-Away and went to bed.

"Ouch!" I stubbed my toe in the dark as I tried to get into bed. I held my breath and listened for Katie. Good, still sleeping.

I often thought about Bill before I went to sleep at night. Sometimes it made me dream of him. I wondered what his bedroom looked like, what he did when he was just hanging around, and what it would be like to kiss him.

Sometimes I was afraid something would happen to me before I ever got kissed by a boy. I could die, in an accident or something, and never even have been on a date! What if nobody ever fell in love with me? I flipped the pillow and stared at the streetlight filtering in through the curtains.

Katie mumbled. I turned over to listen to her. Sometimes she said some pretty neat stuff.

"Angels help," she said dreamily. "Angels help."

I closed my eyes. If you're really there, help me understand, I whispered.

That night I dreamt that I was a queen on a giant chessboard, and every move I made was filled with some deep purpose; maybe not right away, but eventually, all the moves were connected. It was weird. I don't even play chess.

7

Monday afternoon I got off the bus and headed over to Bret Harte. I paused, as I always did, at the big, mahogany doors, to read the motto over the entrance.

Night is too young, O friend! Day is too near;
Wait for the day that maketh all things clear.
Not yet, O friend, not yet!

Bret Harte

When I first came here two years ago, I wondered why they had a motto that the blind kids couldn't even read, but then I found out that all the kids have to memorize it when they first come to the school.

"Good morning, Amelia," said Mrs. Weiss, the

English teacher, as we passed in the main office.

"How'd you know it was me, Mrs. Weiss? I didn't say a word." I threw my junk in the coat closet and went around the counter to my stool.

"You smell like lilacs, dear. You always smell like lilacs." She smiled and gathered her things. "Are you scheduled to help in the main office today?"

"Yes. And I'll take clear, concise phone messages. I've finally got that braille typewriter all figured out, just in time to leave!"

"You've done a good job, and I'll miss your help in my classroom when this year is over. Some of my students have come to think of you as a big sister. You've really made your presence felt here, dear."

"Thanks. Hey, I hear we're in for a long, hot summer."

"Aren't we always?"

I watched her walk to her classroom and marvelled at her unerring sense of direction. It was almost as if the blind each have their own lighthouse in the darkness.

"Hey, how did Helen Keller burn her fingers?"

Mr. Christopher, the principal, stood grinning in front of me. He was tall and lanky, and he had dark hair that was going grey at the temples.

"I don't know," I said patiently. "How did Helen Keller burn her fingers?"

"She was trying to read a waffle iron!"

"Oh, Mr. Christopher, that's awful!" I laughed in spite of myself.

"Yes, I know. But sometimes it's better to laugh in the face of awful. Don't you agree, Miss Fleeman?"

"Yes, Mr. Christopher, I guess I do."

"Would you mind getting me a cup of coffee, and bringing it to my office, Amelia? I want to make a few quick phone calls, and badger people for funding."

"Sure! No problem." I hopped off my stool and ran down to the teachers' lounge.

"Coffee at eleven o'clock, near the phone," I told Mr. C. when I made my delivery. I learned, when I first came to Bret Harte, to use the face of a clock as a guide.

"Thanks. Now I have another request; something has come up suddenly and I need your help."

"Okay."

"We've been assigned our new junior volunteer for next year and I thought you would be the perfect person to show her the ropes. You know, explain the system to her."

"That's okay with me, but I was supposed to work in the main office today."

"Have no fear, I'll hold down the fort, nothing gets past me!"

"I know. You have antennae! So who am I helping?"

"Her name is Vicki Chen and she'll be here," he deftly felt his braille watch, "in five minutes."

"Okay. But first, I have a joke for you."

"Let me have it."

"How did Helen Keller go insane?"

"They put her in charge of a school for the blind?"

"Ha, ha. No. She tried to read the stucco walls!"

He threw his head back and laughed. "That's a new one! I love it!"

I left him chortling to himself while I went to wait for Vicki.

She was right on time and she reminded me of me when I first came: extremely nervous.

"Thank you for helping me. I really hope I can learn everything. Where can we start?" she asked.

"Here, I guess. This is the main office, and Mr. Christopher, the principal, will show you what to do in here later. He'll explain the machines: the Versabrailler, and the enlarging photocopier."

She nodded uncertainly.

"Don't worry, you'll catch on fast. Let's start in the main hallway and work our way back."

"Should I leave my things here?"

"Sure, just stick them in this closet, with my junk." I led the way.

"Why are there lines on the floor?" she asked.

"That's for the kids with low vision. It helps

them make their way in a straight line."

I took Vicki's hand and rubbed it over some strips on the wall near the stairs in the main hall. "These are texture strips for the younger blind kids who need to feel their way along. It warns them the stairs are coming."

"I see." She put her hand to her mouth. "Oh, perhaps that is a bad expression here."

I smiled reassuringly. "No, it's okay. They don't mind that you can see. Sometimes they just mind that they can't.

"Before we go in this kindergarten class, remember you have to say hello and good-bye, so they know for sure who is with them.

"Hi, Mrs. Jones," I called brightly. "Do you mind if I bring the new volunteer through?"

"That's fine, Amelia. You two make yourself useful. We're working on our braille this morning."

"Hi, Amelia!" chirped a small voice to our left. "I love the soap you always use!"

"Hi, Annie! Thanks a lot. I brought someone here today, this is the new helper, Vicki."

"Hi, Vicki." Annie reached her hand out. I took it and gently guided it to Vicki's outstretched hand.

"Amelia, can you help me now? I need powder." Annie rubbed her hands on her dress.

"You remember where it is, don't you?"

"I can't remember."

We went to the supply shelves and I guided her hand to the raised dots for the word powder. Annie applied some to her fingers and went back to her seat.

"The kids can't have hot fingers," I explained quietly, "or they'll stick to the braille paper. And cold fingers can't feel the raised dots. You'll warm up lots of cool hands in the winter and help shake on lots of powder in the summer."

We toured the classrooms and met the teachers, both sighted and blind. Then I took Vicki outside to the play area.

"Hey, Amelia, you're here! I heard your voice!" A chubby, little seven-year-old boy came up and grabbed for my hand.

"Raymond! How's my favorite artist?"

"I'm your favorite?"

"You are!"

"And you're my most beautiful teacher!"

I knelt and hugged him. My tears surprised me.

"Come over to the art table and see my picture."

"Okay."

"Who else is with us, Amelia?"

"Oh, sorry, Ray. This is Vicki, she's the new helper."

"You won't come anymore?"

"Not to help. But I'll come and visit."

He smiled. "Oh, you'll visit and help. I know that!"

We walked over to the outdoor art table. "In the summer the kids do all their art out here. Drawing, clay, painting. The art class is through those big glass doors."

"How do they manage the art?" asked Vicki.

I caught her eye and nodded toward Raymond. She nodded and mouthed, "Okay."

"Raymond, how do you make things in art?" asked Vicki.

"Our art teacher tells us to make what we hear and feel." He held up a bright red scribble. It slashed across the page. "See? Can you tell what it is?"

"Now, I'm not sure, Ray. You help me," I asked.

"Okay. Yesterday we went to the fire station. I saw it there."

"Is it a fire?"

He felt for my ear and held the drawing up close to it. "No! It's the big fire engine. Can't you hear it! That's the *wooo-woooo!*"

"Oh, yes! The siren! I hear it!"

He hugged me and pushed the drawing paper into my hands. "You better take this, so you don't forget."

I hugged him back. "I'll never forget."

"I have to stop and see Mr. C. before I go back to school, Vicki. Next time you come I'll take you to the taping room. You'll get to read books onto tapes for the kids, it's a lot of fun."

"Thank you very much. This was very helpful. You enjoy it here, don't you?"

"I love it here!" I said.

"You are so sure of yourself. I hope I can do as good as you."

"Oh, well, I never thought of it like that." I hurried back to the main office.

"Got a minute?" I asked, after tapping on Mr. Christopher's door.

"I have many. Why, for you, Amelia, I have a veritable plethora of minutes! Have a seat."

"Okay, good. I only need a few, though."

"Of course, the ever-efficient Amelia, things to do, people to help. How'd Vicki do?"

"Great. She'll fit right in. There's something else . . ."

"What's up?"

"Well, I have sort of a . . . it's not a big present, just something I want to give you before I have to leave here."

"Why, Amelia, I'm touched. Truly." He grinned. "And I love presents."

"It's a taped radio broadcast of 'The Miracle Worker.' It reminds me of what you do here." I slid it across the desk.

He picked it up and turned it over in his hands.

"This means a great deal to me, Amelia. And I thank you."

"You're welcome."

He reached behind him for a tissue and handed it to me.

"I didn't make a peep! How'd you know?"

"I hear the tears, my dear."

I tried to blow discreetly. "Well, I'd better be going . . ."

"Amelia, before you go . . ."

"Yes?"

"I'll treasure this taped story of Helen Keller and her teacher. I know I make a lot of Helen Keller jokes, but I actually admire her a great deal."

"Oh, sure, I know."

"Have you ever read her autobiography?"

"No."

"It's a joy." He leaned back and cradled his head in his hands. "Once, someone asked Helen, if she could have one of her senses restored, which would it be: hearing or vision? Which do you think she chose?"

"Well, if it was me," I sniffed and wiped my nose. "I think I'd rather be deaf than blind, because then I could still get around by myself, and read regular books, and see faces, and everything."

"Well, Helen chose the opposite. She said she would rather be blind, because hearing is the more powerful sense. You can tell a great deal about a person if you close your eyes. You aren't swayed by how things look. You hear the truth about them." He suddenly leaned forward across the desk. "That's what I want you to take from here."

"I think I understand."

I signed out and walked into the sunshine, across the alley that separated the two schools. It was more than an alley, though; it was the vast expanse between two different worlds. And I wasn't sure which one was really in the dark.

When I got home from school I found Kate watching cartoons and painting her toenails different colors with her magic markers.

"Some lady just called for you, Amelia."

"Did you take a message?"

"I told Cyril to."

"Then where is it?"

"He couldn't. He was in the middle of helping me plan my birthday. It's okay, she'll call later."

"What's with your birthday? It's months away."

"You see, I want to go on the Graveline Tour. It costs a lot, so I have to plan."

"You mean *Gray*line, like the stars' homes?"

"Noooo. I mean *Grave*. I saw a commercial for it. They take you on a tour all over Hollywood in a real death car so—"

"Not a death car, it's called a hearse."

"Whatever. Anyway, then you look at all the

places where famous people died. Or got murdered! Then you go see where they're buried."

"That would be a pretty creepy party for an eight-year-old, don't you think?"

"Eight has nothing to do with it. And I would be nine by then. It's not creepy, either. Those people aren't in their graves. Just their leftovers are there."

"Leftovers? Sounds like an old roast chicken dinner to me!"

"Shows what you know. Cyril says graves are for the living. The dead have all moved on."

"He ought to know!"

She swatted at me, and I jumped away to answer the phone.

"*I'll* get it this time!" I ran to the kitchen. "Hello?"

"Good afternoon. May I please speak with Amelia Fleeman?"

"This is me, I mean she."

"Amelia, this is Rebecca Britton. I've been trying to get in touch with you."

"Yes?"

"I'm Candy Crowley's personal secretary."

8

I gripped the edge of the kitchen counter.

"Are you still there, Amelia?"

"Yes, I'm here."

"I have a suggestion card in front of me, which was signed by you. Do you recall filling one out when you were in the studio audience?"

"Y-y-yes."

"Good. We're moving right along then. I was impressed with what you wrote, so I showed it to Candy, and she agreed with me. We want you to be on the show!"

"Are you kidding? Me? Why come? I mean how for? Oh, geez! I mean why?"

"Because we think we can build a show around the theme of your card."

"Wow. My card had a theme?"

She laughed. "Yes, it did to us. And we know the show will be more powerful if you are a guest. Since your address was local, we decided to ask. Of course, you need your parents' permission."

"I know my mom will say it's okay. And my little sister will die. She'll have a cow! I was just sort of messing around; I never thought you'd pay attention to that card."

"Actually, it kind of jumped out at me."

"I'm so glad it did!"

"I can tell! Anyway, Candy agrees with you that girls in this country are pressured to be perfect and skinny and sexy. She wants to call the show "Pressured To Be Perfect." Can you be there?"

"*Yes!* Just tell me when and what I need to do."

"Okay, first I'll overnight the release for a parent to sign and mail back, then this Friday we'll send a limo to your house around noon to pick you up. We tape at four. That gives you time to meet Candy, go to makeup, and get psyched. We'll have reserved seats for your family in the front row. Do I have an okay from you?"

"You have a gigantic okay!"

"Great! Keep those enthusiasm levels up, and I'll see you this Friday. I look forward to meeting you, Amelia! Good-bye."

"Bye!"

I turned around to scream for Kate, but she was in front of me.

"Cyril just told me. I can't believe it, either!"

That night I called Shura.

"Guess what?"

"What?"

"No, guess!"

"Just tell me, Amelia, it'll save time. I've still got to practice the piano tonight."

"You're such a fud, but okay, I'll tell you. I, your best friend, Amelia Mildred Fleeman, am going to be on the Candy K. Crowley show!"

"No way!!"

"Yes way! We're taping this Friday afternoon." I explained the whole suggestion card thing.

"Hey, that is so cool, Amelia, I'm so happy for you. Are you nervous?"

"At first I was too shocked to think. Now I've moved on to scared spitless, and I guess petrified is next. I'm trying not to think about it too much, it makes my stomach go all knotty.

"But first of all, I have to buy something to wear, Mom said so. She's going to give me money for a graduation dress, and she says to wear the same thing on the show. You want to come shopping with me tomorrow after school?"

"Sure, you want to take the bus over to the Galleria?"

"That'd be great. I'll see you tomorrow!"

"Amelia?"

"Yeah?"

"This really *is* a BFD!"

"I know it, Shur."

"One more thing . . ."

"What?"

"Can I have your autograph?"

"Ha, ha."

I went to the P.E. closet and got out the orange cones for flag football.

"Hey, Amelia, I just heard the big news! Aren't you excited? I'd love to meet Candy Crowley, she is so cool!" Rosalinda Rodriguez carefully removed her dangly earrings and put them in her pocket. No jewelry allowed during P.E.

"How'd you hear, Rosa?"

"Shura mentioned it this morning to a teacher, and I overheard her."

"Does everybody know now?" I yanked the bag of balls out of the closet.

"I only told a couple of people, but you know how that goes!" She giggled. "My mom says, telephone, telegraph, tele-Rosa!"

"News whips around this school on fast forward." I shut the door. "We better go, or we'll be late for P.E."

"So what are you going to talk about? How come

they asked you to be on the show?" She followed me outside to the field, where we lined up to wait for Miss Knight, the P.E. teacher.

Every single girl out there swarmed up and buzzed around me as if I were the hive!

"Who asked you to be on?"

"Can you get me Candy's autograph?"

"Are you allowed to bring guests?"

The questions came fast and furious until Miss Knight blew her whistle, good and loud—twice.

"Ladies, ladies, please get in your proper lines and count off. I know we have a celebrity in our midst, but we have stretches to do and balls to volley! Abrams, count off!"

After P.E. we had lunch. Shura and I usually met at the cafeteria and sat alone on a bench under a tree on the quad. Not today. Suddenly, every girl in the school seemed to remember my name!

"Geez, this is like trying to eat lunch with Madonna!" groaned Shura as the girls crowded around and called out questions. She waved her hand in the air, but they ignored her. "Hey!" she yelled.

Silence fell.

"That's better. My friend, Amelia, will be happy to answer your questions. But I will act as her press secretary, and choose one of you at a time. Raise your hands, or I won't call on you."

I smiled. Leave it to Shura to take charge of all BFDs.

"Okay, Rosa, ask."

"How did you get to be on the show?"

"I took my little sister to see a taping and they asked for suggestions. I guess they liked mine, so they asked me to come on and talk about it."

Shura pointed to the back of the pack. "Back there. Yeah, you."

"Are you really going to talk about feeling like you're not pretty?"

"Yes."

"Won't you be, like, mortified?"

"No more than usual."

A bunch of people laughed.

"In fact," I said. "How many of *you* guys feel like you're not really pretty enough?"

Slowly hands went up, one by one. Almost every one. I was amazed.

After school I hurried down the hall so I could meet Shura and go shopping. I stopped to heave my backpack higher on my shoulder and felt somebody pat my behind. I jumped a mile.

"Hey, Cornelia, what's this I hear about you being on the tube?"

I looked around at Bill and swallowed hard. "I'm Amelia."

"Oh, that's right, Amelia." He grinned and

leaned against the wall. "You forgive me, don't you?"

"Sure."

"So, that's pretty cool. I heard you were supposed to talk about being plain, or something. Is that right?"

"Well, yeah, mostly." I found an interesting ceiling crack to stare at. "I guess that sounds weird to you."

"No. It's not weird. I can see how you'd feel plain. I don't mean that in a creepy way or anything."

"Of course not. Listen, I need to go now, I'm meeting a friend." I started to walk away.

"Hey, wait, can you get Candy Crowley's autograph for me? I know this girl who really loves her show. I could really make points with her."

"No. I'm sorry. I won't do that; it wouldn't be polite. See ya, Bill."

I liked him better in my dreams.

The bus was hot and crowded when Shura and I took off after school. It was a pleasure to get into the air-conditioned comfort of the three-story Galleria Mall.

"We have looked at every dress in every store," said Shura after two hours of shopping. "I want to sit down." She headed for the food court. "Let's get a drink, okay?"

"Okay. I know it's taking a long time, but nothing looks right on me." I plopped down in a seat and dug around in my purse for some change. "Are you getting in line? If you are, get me a Coke, will you?"

"Caffeine is bad for you."

"I don't care. You should be glad it's the only drug I take."

"All right, all right. Think about that dark purple dress, will you? I thought it looked really good on you."

"I looked like a velvet grape."

She sighed and got in line.

"Listen," I said when she got back. "I think we missed that new little shop on the third level. It's called Moonglow or Moonstruck or something."

"It's kind of a hippie place, isn't it?"

"So?" I sucked on my straw.

"Hey, I don't care. I just thought maybe you'd want to dress conservatively. You usually do."

"I know it, but I've decided that this would be a good time to try something different. I want a dress that says *me* when I look at it. Most of my clothes seem to say, *who?*"

And that's exactly what I found at Moonglow. It might not make the cover of *Seventeen,* but it said Amelia.

"Before we eat, I want to see your new dress," called Mom from her room.

"Okay!" I slipped it on and went in to model it for her. "Here it is! What do you think?"

"Oooooooh, I love it!" said Katie, who was reading on Mom's bed.

"It is perfect, Amelia! What an unusual choice!"

"It's not too unusual, is it?" I fingered the soft, deep blue material, and gazed at the little crescent moons that decorated the hem. "I don't want to look like a space cadet."

"You don't," said Kate matter-of-factly. "Cyril says you look celestial!"

"For once," said Mom with a smile, "I agree with Cyril. I think the moon motif is a nice touch. Go in my bathroom and look in my full-length mirror. You know what? You remind me of Loretta Young in *The Bishop's Wife*."

"Which old movie is that?" I asked from the bathroom.

"Oh, it's about an angel, played by Cary Grant, who comes to help this woman when she's in trouble. It's a nice fantasy."

"That's what you think," said Kate. "Angels help people all the time.

I gazed in the mirror, hoping for an angel to appear. But all I could see was me.

9

By Thursday afternoon I was a nervous wreck. Only one more day until the Candy Crowley show. I sat in Math and stared at the clock.

We were supposed to learn factoring, but it was going right over my head—*whoosh!*

"Wake up!" I felt a familiar poke. "He asked you for the answer," whispered Richard.

"I'm not sure if I understand that part, Mr. Jacobs." I tried to fake it.

"Miss Fleeman, I know stardom beckons, but you don't want to miss these principles, they *will* come back to haunt you." He waved his pointer at me. "Factoring is not something to let slide by while you daydream."

"Sorry. I'm listening now." I sat up straighter

and stared at the numbers dancing across the board. It was Greek to me!

The bell finally rang and I packed my stuff in my backpack. I'd need a math tutor, for sure, before the test.

I hoisted the pack to my left shoulder and started out the door.

"Amelia! Wait up!"

"Oh, Richard, thanks a lot for trying to warn me back there."

"Sure." He pushed his glasses up and fell into step beside me.

"Did you want something?"

"Sort of. Will you meet me in the library in ten minutes?"

I furrowed my brow. "Why?"

"I'll tell you in the library. Will you come?"

"Okay, but I only have a few minutes. I'm meeting a girl over at Bret Harte at three-thirty."

" 'Tis possible that so short a time can alter the condition of a man.' "

I turned and looked at him. "What?"

"Nothing. I was just barding around. I'll see you there after I hit the bathroom."

"Okay."

The library was empty, except for the librarian. She stopped filing and nodded at me when I came

81

in. I spotted Richard in the far corner, near the windows.

"Hi." I set my backpack on the table. "What's up?"

"My courage, I hope," he mumbled. He pushed his glasses up and brushed the hair out of his eyes. He dropped his pencil, bent to retrieve it, and knocked his notebook and papers to the floor.

"Shhhhh," warned the librarian.

"Richard, you are acting so weird," I whispered as I helped him pick up his stuff. "Are you okay?" I sat down across from him and waited for him to say something.

"Hey, what's with this table?" I grabbed the edges. "It feels like we're having an earthquake in here."

"Oh." The shaking stopped. "I was bouncing my knee. Rather forcefully."

"Rather." I smiled at him.

"You, ah, ready for your television debut?"

"No. Couldn't you tell in class? I'm getting more nervous by the minute. Is that why you asked me here? Do you have some tips on how I can be more relaxed or something?"

"*Me?*" his voice cracked.

I pretended not to notice.

He shook his head. "I'm afraid being relaxed is not on my agenda at the moment. Boy, it's hot in here."

"Ah, not really. This *is* the only air-conditioned room in the whole school."

"Oh."

I looked out the window and waited. I read a few book titles behind his head. My eyes roamed over to the bulletin board. There was a notice about not eating in the library, a schedule for tutorials, and then a big, blue and gold announcement about the graduation dance. The dance! Oh, no! Is that what this was all about? Was he going to ask me?

He cleared his throat. "I guess, now that you're going on TV, a lot of guys have been calling you, maybe even asked you to the dance . . . ?" His voice trailed off and he met my eyes for a split second.

"No, no one has called yet . . ." I'd prayed to be asked, but I didn't expect Richard Flink to be the answer!

"Well?"

"Well, what?" I stalled.

"Will you go with me? To the graduation dance?"

"Um, I don't know, I'm not sure what my plans are . . . exactly . . ."

"Amelia . . . just . . . hear me out."

I looked up. He looked scared. I cradled my forehead in one hand and stared down at the table. Then I closed my eyes and listened.

"Okay. Here's the deal. I know I'm not exactly Prince Charming. In fact, one girl informed me that I'm Prince Charmless. But I'm not asking you to get married here. Just go to a dance. We can go together and see what it's like; I've never been to one. I want to go with you because we're friends."

I felt his anxiety and I felt how much courage it took to ask.

I blinked back the tears, looked up, and gave him my best smile. "I don't have any exact plans, so I'd really like to go with you, Richard. I'm so glad you asked me."

"You are? You will?" He smiled and looked closely at me. " 'Sunshine and rain at once; her smiles and tears.' Don't worry, Amelia. We'll have a good time, I promise!"

"I'm not worried about the dance. Really. I'm worried about being on the Candy Crowley show."

"Think positively. Imagine it all working out the way you want."

"That works?"

He grinned. "Worked for me!"

"Here I am, Vicki. Sorry I'm a little late!"

"No problem, Mr. Christopher showed me all the machines. He is a very funny man! I think helping here will be a nice thing for me."

"I know it will! Come on, I need to finish the book I'm reading onto tape, and I thought it would be good for you to see exactly how it works."

"Can you tell me," she asked as we walked, "why the younger blind children sometimes smile and rock back and forth? And they have funny expressions, too."

"That's because they can't see themselves. They have to learn how they look to sighted people. They can't mimic like we can. We're supposed to remind them to look at us when they speak and to sit up straight, and 'hold their faces quiet' as they say here."

"It must be hard work for them. I hope to help."

"You'll do real well," I said. "I can tell."

She smiled.

"Okay, here we are, the soundproof recording room. Always be sure the door is closed."

After I showed Vicki how to run the equipment, I settled in front of the microphone. "Don't worry if you make a few mistakes. I made lots at first. Once, I kept sipping water while I read and you could hear it on the tape. Mr. Christopher said it sounded like bath water sloshing around. Another time I was making my shoes come off my heels, and the tape picked that up. It's really sensitive, so if you need to sneeze or drink, or anything like that, just stop the tape."

"Thanks for warning me."

I opened *The Velveteen Rabbit*, and continued reading the story where I had left off.

Generally, by the time you are Real, most of your hair has been loved off, and your eyes drop out and you get loose in the joints and very shabby. But these things don't matter at all, because when you are Real, you can't be ugly, except to people who don't understand . . .

Kate pounced on me as soon as I hit the front door.

"Cyril told me you'd be going to a dance. He told me! I already knew it!"

"You have *got* to be kidding me!"

"No! I'm not kidding. So, when the boy called, I knew it already!"

"Richard called?"

"Yep. He'll call back. He wants to know the color of your dress!"

"My dress?"

"For the dance, silly! His mom said he's s'posed to buy you a flower."

"Wow. A corsage."

"Then Mommy called to be sure I was home okay and already in the house. And I told her. She was so happy! She said you can have another new dress. Special, for the dance!"

"Well, you can remember messages when you want to, can't you?"

"*And,* Mommy says she's coming home a little early to hear all about it. You are so lucky, Melia."

I hugged her. "Maybe I am."

"Know what else? The boy, Richard? I told him I was home with Cyril."

"You did, huh? What did he think of that?"

"He said when he was little, he had a Cyril, too. Only his was named Wally. So he was never lonely either."

I hugged her tighter. "I think it's nice that you have Cyril. I'm sorry that I've always given you such a hard time about him."

"Oh, that's okay. You can't help it. It's just because you don't know your angel yet. That's all."

"How about a game of Scrabble Junior?" I tousled her hair.

"Goody!" She jumped up and then stopped in her tracks. "No, that's okay, Cyril. I think I'll try it by myself this time."

10

By Friday morning I was a complete zombie. It had finally and truly sunken in that I would be on national television. A kazillion people would watch me talk about being plain in a pretty world. Me, Amelia Mildred Fleeman, that nice, quiet girl with glasses and a furrowed brow, on the Candy K. Crowley show!

"*Mom!* My hair looks awful! Help! It won't do anything I want it to! I wish I had thick hair like you!" I gave the brush a frustrated fling and it landed with a clatter in the shower stall.

"Good heavens, Amelia, I've never seen you like this! Try to calm yourself! You're just nervous." Mom appeared behind me in the mirror. "It looks fine. I'm sure if it needs a little something, the staff on the show will take care of it. Just go pick up the hairbrush, settle down, and let me see what I can do for now."

Kate peeked in. "Cyril says it's more important what's in your head than what's on it."

"And I bet Cyril is bald!" I said. I smiled in spite of my nervousness.

"Is not. He has nice, wavy brown hair and he wears a hat. He always tips his hat, too. The people who can see him always smile and nod back."

"Katie, sweetie, will you go and wait in the living room? That's a good girl. Don't muss your dress."

"Okay, Mommy. But Cyril says for Melia to stop expecting disaster. He says she practically invites it in for a cup of tea!"

"That's pretty cute," Mom said with a chuckle. "I wonder where on earth she comes up with it!"

At exactly twelve noon the limo arrived. A tall man in a black suit and a cap with CBS STUDIOS on the front knocked on the door. I opened it. "Is this the Fleeman residence?" he asked.

I was tongue-tied. No, I was tongue-knotted! I stared at him.

"Oh, yes!" said Mom, coming to the rescue. "That's us!"

We followed him outside and the neighbors cheered and whistled. Mom and Kate waved and I walked woodenly toward the waiting limousine. I passed the Tiki and rubbed his tummy. Couldn't hurt.

"So, this is how it looks inside one of these stretch limos, I've always been curious," said Mom as she settled back into the air-conditioned comfort and thick, leather seats. "Wait until the girls at work hear what this was like! The nurses' station will be buzzing!"

"Oh, looky! A baby refrigerator right in the car!" Kate opened the mini-fridge door and we gazed at the cool drinks and snacks.

"Excuse me, ladies," came a voice from beyond.

We all jumped and Mom slammed the little door.

"Don't worry! It's just me, Roger, up front. Miss Crowley wants you to help yourselves to anything you'd like back there. We'll be about thirty minutes en route, unless there's a snag on the freeway. Eat, drink, and be merry!"

Mom found a little red button near a speaker and pushed it. "Thank you very much, Roger, we are very merry!"

We looked at each other and cracked up. I'm sure he thought we were nuts!

"How are you holding up?" Mom smoothed my dress, but not my nerves.

"Okay, I guess. Sorry about throwing the brush around the bathroom. I guess I was taking out my anxiety on my hair. I can't help thinking of how many millions of people will see this thing."

"Try not to dwell on that, kiddo. Just think of it as talking to Shura. Pretend Candy Crowley is Shura."

"Yeah," said Kate seriously. "Except Candy never says BFD."

"What *does* that mean, anyway?" asked Mom.

"You don't really want to know, Mom . . . about the show today, I guess I'm worried because I don't know what she'll ask. I don't want to sound like a fruitcake."

"How could you? You're too smart for that."

"I don't feel smart. I feel scared."

"Row, row, row your boat, gently down the stream . . ." sang Kate. Off-key.

"Kate, not now," I pleaded.

"We sing that at school. Teacher told me it means to go with the current. You know, like when I put my popsicle sticks in the gutter water. They just float along to the sea." She made wave motions with her hands.

"Yeah, right. Unless they get stuck in the sewer first."

Kate laughed. "Melia you're so funny!"

"I know. I'm hysterical. I hope I don't barf."

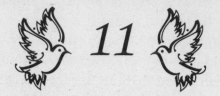

11

"Okay, end of the line, ladies!" said Roger. "The famous CBS studios are right here." He swung into a reserved parking space, jumped out, and opened our door.

"I feel like a queen," said Mom.

"I feel like a princess," said Kate.

"I feel sick," I said.

"This must be the guest star," Roger said with a grin. "They're always the green ones. And that's where you'll go pretty soon—to the greenroom." He gestured to a guard. "Okay, Jack, get these ladies safely to Miss Britton, she'll take over from here."

Jack nodded and led us silently inside.

"Hi! You must be Amelia! I'm Rebecca Britton, re-member me? I'm the one who got you into this!" A tall, well-dressed, redhead extended her hand.

Zombie-woman stared at her.

Mom stepped in. "So nice to meet you, Miss Britton. I'm Frances Fleeman, and these are my daughters, Kate and Amelia."

Miss Britton shook Mom's hand.

"We'll take good care of her, Mrs. Fleeman. And in the meantime, I'll have one of the pages show you and Kate around the studio, and then to your seats. How's that sound?"

"Cool!" said Kate.

Mom kissed me. "Break a leg, kiddo!"

I watched them walk away. My stomach lurched. "Miss Britton, I think I might be sick," I whispered.

She got me to the ladies room just in time.

"I hear you had a date with the porcelain god!"

"I am so embarrassed." I looked up at Candy Crowley and smiled wanly.

"Don't be. I still toss the old cookies now and then. You'll be fine." She sat next to me on the couch in the greenroom. "Only fifteen minutes until the show starts. Do you have any last minute questions?"

"No questions. Miss Britton explained everything." I smoothed my dress and remembered not to touch my face. The makeup lady had put powder on me so I wouldn't shine in the bright television lights. "I'm not too nervous now, Miss Crowley, it's getting better. I just feel kind of numb."

"That sounds about right. I feel numb before every taping, and then some weird energy kicks in and I just sort of float right through it. Although, I guess it could be all those donuts I eat while we're pulling the show together!" She laughed and tossed her blunt-cut, shoulder length, black hair back. Her jewelry caught my eye.

"I really like your necklace with the kiss charm, Miss Crowley. I noticed how you always wear it on the show."

"I wish you'd call me Candy, and yes, I always wear my little kiss necklace. I wanted to wear something special, something that had meaning for me. Kind of a talisman."

"A talisman?"

"Mmmm-hmmm. A talisman is sort of a magic symbol that brings good luck to the person wearing it."

"That little kiss charm is magic?"

"Sure. As long as I believe it is." She gave her kiss a kiss and smiled.

Rebecca Britton hurried in clutching a clipboard. "Come on, Candy Dandy, time to get settled on the set and do a little audience warm-up." Miss Britton turned to me with a big smile. "Don't worry about your mother and sister, Amelia. I have them all cozied up in the first row."

I nodded numbly. Candy patted my hand and left.

"You're about as green as this room!" said Miss Britton. "Don't sweat it, Amelia, you'll be great. You just sit tight. I'll come and get you and walk you to the curtain when it's time for you to go on. Just relax until then! Or at least try to." She closed the door with a smile.

"Relax! Hah!" I said out loud to myself. I paced up and down the room. I prayed my pimples didn't show up.

Suddenly, I realized I wasn't alone. There was a lady in a long white dress, standing in the far corner. I smiled at her. "I'm real nervous," I said. "I wish I didn't have to go out there all by myself."

"Not to worry, dear. Everything will be fine. You know, you are never really alone. I am always at your side." She tilted her head and smiled at me.

Something about her made me want to listen to her lyrical voice and believe her comforting words, even though I didn't have a clue as to what she was talking about!

I smiled back. "What exactly do you mean about not being alone, because I am—"

I stopped and turned toward Rebecca Britton who hurried back into the greenroom and seated a small, well-dressed lady on the couch, then she gestured at me. "Okay, Amelia. Move it or lose it! It's show time!"

I forgot about the lady in white as I followed Miss Britton woodenly down a number of hallways. We ended up behind a heavy, blue curtain. There were wires, ropes, and people hanging around all over the place. I never realized how much goes on behind the scenes!

"And here she is, our own Candy Kiss!" yelled the announcer.

Applause rose and fell, then Candy explained about my suggestion card, and introduced me. My knees felt like Slinkys.

"Give 'em hell, Amelia!" said Miss Britton as she pulled back the curtain and gave me a little push into the hot, bright lights.

Applause hit me in the face and then washed over me like a shower. I spotted Mom and Kate in the front row, beaming and clapping. I took a deep breath and out I went!

Candy seated me and clipped a microphone to my clothes. "So, Amelia. First of all, I thought I would read your suggestion card. Is that okay with you?"

"Sure," I croaked. Be an actress, be an actress, I reminded myself silently.

"Let's give our young guest a moment to take a little drink." She smiled reassuringly at me and picked my card out of the stack of papers on her lap.

I sipped water and tensed my shaking knees.

"We give out these little cards at all of our tapings and we encourage our audience members to share ideas and suggestions. Here is Amelia's.

"I would like to suggest that you do a show about being not so pretty. I mean, about girls who are plain and have to live in a pretty world, like Hollywood. I think these girls should not always be on make-over shows. I think you should talk about their feelings, instead of cover it all up with make-up. Thank you very much. Amelia Fleeman. Age 12 (almost 13).'"

The audience was quiet for a minute. Then they all clapped. It was louder than when I first came out.

"That's what we thought, too." She turned to me. "It was a very good idea. So, no make-over today, right?"

I nodded.

"Have you always felt plain, Amelia?"

I swallowed and nodded. Boy, I was really wowing them!

"Since you were . . . ?"

I cleared my throat. "Ever since I was about five, I guess."

"Did something happen then?"

"Yes. School happened."

The audience laughed.

"Yeah," said Candy. "School can be tough. What happened at school?"

"Well. Boys make jokes about who is pretty and who is ugly. And the other girls make fun if you don't wear the popular outfits. It starts out slow in kindergarten, but it gets a lot worse. And I still have to face junior high!"

"I hear you, girl. I was called Howley for years. They said I was a werewolf because I had hairy arms."

"Really? I can't imagine that happening to *you*!"

"Well, it's true. So, you're not alone."

"I kind of knew that. I heard them call other girls names, and do mean things."

"What kind of mean things?"

"Well, one time I remember is just at the beginning of sixth grade. We were all in the cafeteria for lunch, and a whole table of boys made up signs with numbers on them and they held up a number for each girl as she came out of the lunch line. It was awful!"

"You mean, like in the Olympics? Where the best is a ten, and so on, down to one?"

"Uh-huh."

"Do you want to say what number you got, and how you felt?"

"I got a one-and-a-half. I wanted to die! I wished a hole would open in the floor and swallow me up.

And after that, the girls who were tens avoided the girls who were ones."

"I've been there, too, honey. Sometimes we gals are awful hard on each other. I bet half the women in this audience have felt it, in one way or another."

The women in the audience clapped real loud. It sure sounded like more than half.

Candy waited for them to stop. "So, it got worse as you got older?"

"Yes."

"Like what?"

"Well, like, ah, developing. Or, you know, not."

Candy shook her head. "I don't get your drift."

Someone in the audience called out, "Big boobs or little boobs, Candy!"

"You see, that's why I need my audience," said Candy. "They are way ahead of me!"

Laughter rolled over the room.

"Okay, so there is more to make fun of as you get older, right?"

"Yes. They talk about who has the biggest chest. A lot. Boys snapped the back of my bra and asked me why I bothered. They said a couple of Band-Aids would work. Girls do it too, though. They just don't say it directly to your face."

"But you know, don't you? You can feel it."

"I don't think they care. Maybe they think other people don't have feelings or something."

"So do you think that's why you feel plain?"

"Partly. I guess it also has to do with the way women look on TV and in the movies and magazines and stuff."

"They look perfect," said Candy. "Gorgeous and skinny." Candy made a face and patted her tummy. She was not too skinny.

"My mom told me that there used to be a model named Twiggy and that she really was about as big as a twig."

"Oh, don't get me started on Twiggy!" said Candy. "That will have to be on our show about anorexia!"

The audience clapped, and Candy broke for a commercial.

I sipped my water and looked over at Mom. She smiled and gave me a wave. Kate bounced in her seat and stared at the lights and cameras.

Candy leaned in and whispered, "You are doing great, Amelia! How do you feel?"

"Okay, I guess."

"I'll take questions from the audience in the next segment, then we'll break for commercial, and our next guest will join us."

"Who else is on?"

"Dr. Karen Barnes. She wrote a book called *Pretty At All Costs*. You probably saw her in the greenroom. Miss Britton took her in there just before you came out."

I nodded and wondered who the third lady in the greenroom had been, then the theme music rose up. Candy positioned herself in the audience.

The first question came from an older lady. "Hello, Candy. I just love your show, honey."

"Thank you so much. Did you want to ask something?"

"Oh, yes. I think magazines and TV encourage girls to try to look older than they are, do you think that's true, Amelia?"

I thought for a minute. "Yes. I remember when I turned eleven, the crowd of popular girls made fun of me because I didn't have my ears pierced yet, or wear makeup. I probably would have, just to fit in, but my mom wouldn't let me."

"Good for your mother," said the lady.

The audience clapped and Mom grinned like the Cheshire Cat when the camera pointed her way. Candy ran around for another question.

"Yes, young man, what's your question?" she asked.

He tugged on his baseball cap. "Well, I just think that some girls are pretty and some aren't. And the ones who aren't should just learn to deal with it, you know? Guys want to date the good-looking chicks, with that long, curly hair."

"That long, curly hair takes hours of upkeep," said Candy. She looked at me. "You want to say anything to Mr. Baseball Cap here?"

"Yes. I want to say that I could deal with it a whole lot easier if people didn't go around acting like the only thing that matters is your face. *And* it's more important what's in your head than what's on it!"

"Listen," Candy gave him a poke. "You aren't exactly some prize peacock yourself, you know that?"

The audience laughed and applauded. The guy sat down with a shrug.

"Okay, one more, then we have to break. They're giving me the cut sign," said Candy.

"Yes, over here, Candy!" called an older woman who was waving her hat in the air. She grabbed the mike when Candy got to her. "I've been around a long time and I've seen stars come and go. One year they're skinny as rails, the next they're big bosomed, and now they seem to be weight lifters. It changes like the seasons. Have you noticed that?"

"I think I know what you mean. I like to watch old movies with my mom, and I noticed that the female stars change a lot more than the men. One year it looked like it was popular to paint on eyebrows halfway up your forehead!"

Everyone laughed.

"That's right," said Candy. "I remember my grandmother talking about binding her breasts during the 1920s, so she could be flat, which was all the rage then! My! How things change! Just ask the plastic surgeons!"

The official applause sign went on and we went to commercial.

"This is going really well, Amelia. You can relax a little bit now. Dr. Barnes is up next."

"Whew!" I took a deep breath. "Okay." I wondered if the perspiration showed on my dress.

The rest of the show was about Dr. Barnes' book, *Pretty At All Costs*. Candy held it up a lot and Dr. Barnes quoted from it a lot.

It was a book about how lots of young girls don't feel too good about themselves, and what they could do to feel better. Maybe I would read it over the summer.

At the end of the show Candy held up the book again. "And let's also have a round of applause for Amelia Fleeman. I think she's one of the bravest girls I've ever met!"

The audience clapped and clapped.

Mom cried.

After the show we went out for dinner to celebrate. We ate, hashed over the show, and strolled through the Galleria Mall.

"Let's go over to the bookstore," said Mom. "I want to read that new biography of Charlie Chaplin, and I want to buy Dr. Barnes' book for you girls."

"Yeah, and I want to get the next book in the *Little House* series." Kate tugged on Mom's hand. "Let's go!"

"Coming, Amelia?" asked Mom.

"In a minute, Mom. I want to look in the jewelry store first. I'll meet you guys in the bookstore in a few minutes." I strolled over to Henson's Jewelry.

"May I help you select some item of jewelry, young lady?" asked the dapper, wavy-haired man behind the well-cleaned, glass counter.

"Well, maybe." I tapped my fingers on the glass. "I'm looking for some special piece of jewelry to wear. Like a necklace, or maybe a bracelet. Something different. Sort of a talisman."

He thought for a moment. "Well, perhaps you'd be interested in one of these." He pulled out a tray of little golden angels. "These are quite popular." He removed one. "They are, as you can see, miniature angels. They are actually small pins to be worn on the shoulder, to remind the wearer of his or her guardian angel. Rather amusing, don't you think? Would you care to purchase one?"

"No, thank you. That's not what I had in mind." I turned to go, then paused. "Besides, I don't think you can buy angels."

"Of course not. At least, not the real ones. We're not for sale."

I looked up, startled. "What did you—"

"*They're* not for sale. That's what I meant to say,

of course." He leaned toward me and smiled.

"Of course." I stared at him for a minute, then hurried out to find Mom and Kate.

A voice whispered in my ear, "Cyril is such a kidder."

I jumped and looked quickly to my left.

I appeared to be alone.

Boy, it had been a long, weird day.

12

HIGHLAND GRADE SCHOOL GRADUATION read the wrinkled program in my sweaty hand.

I shook my head and tried to pay attention to the boring speaker. He was yapping about our next big adventure: Junior High. Why did adults always refer to things as adventures?

"And so, as you leave the halls of Highland, the home of the blue and gold, may you take the lessons learned here and use them as a springboard to your further education in our fine school system."

Somebody behind me made snoring noises. Loud. We all giggled.

Boring guy number three finally sat down and we offered a hot, half-hearted smattering of applause.

I looked at my watch. This should be winding up, all that was left to do was the class awards.

Our principal, Mrs. Perez, read off the awards. The usual people won the big stuff. I saw Mr. Lockwood run up with a video camera and capture the big moment when Wendy won "Most Popular." Again.

I won an attendance award and an honor roll award.

Then Mr. Christopher came to the mike.

"We at Bret Harte would like to thank all of you here at Highland for helping to make the inclusion program between our two schools work as well as it has. We appreciate the climate of acceptance we have felt from all of you."

Everyone clapped.

"And, finally, we want to honor a young lady who has meant a great deal to us at Bret Harte." He reached behind him and pulled something out of a box. It hung from a thin, blue ribbon. "Will Amelia Fleeman please come up here? Come on, Amelia, I know you're out there; you can't hide from me!"

People chuckled and looked around. I felt a poke.

"Amelia, he's talking about you. You better wake up enough to walk, I don't want you to trip and break an ankle! I've waited too long for our date!"

I turned and smiled gratefully at Richard and stood up. People around me clapped. I made my way to the stage in a bit of a daze.

"Here she is," said Mr. Christopher. "I know it's her because she always smells like lilacs. How are you, Amelia?"

"Surprised."

"Good. That means my students can keep a secret." He adjusted the mike. "Amelia Fleeman has been a volunteer at my school for two years now. And in that time she has been a hard-working, pleasant, and enthusiastic addition to our family of students. The members of our student body have voted her a special award, which I now present." He turned to me. "Amelia, this was designed for you in art class by the younger students and executed in silver by the older ones. I present it on their behalf." He dangled it in the air and I let it settle in my palm.

It was a circular medal with lilacs engraved on one side. I turned it over and read, "Wait for the day that maketh all things clear." I ran my fingertips over the familiar words.

"It is so beautiful. Thank you. Very much. It's the nicest award I ever received, in fact, it's the only one. . . ." I started to cry and Mr. C. gave me a hug.

I headed back to my seat, accepting congratulations as I went, then we sang the school song, and the ceremony was over. We were free! Until September, anyway.

After that it was insane. Parents, cameras, kids

and blue and gold balloons were everywhere. Girls were kicking off their high heels and boys were ripping off their ties.

Richard tapped me on the shoulder and handed me a present. "A little something I slaved over."

"Oh, Richard, I didn't get anything for you . . ."

"Open it! Come on!"

I tore into the flowered paper. "This is so nice! Did you make it yourself?" I turned the wooden box over in my hands. "It's so smooth."

"Rough edges are easy to smooth with an electric sander." He grinned. "My mom thought you could keep jewelry in it, or something."

"She's right, I will. Is she here? I'd love to meet her."

"Good. Because she's coming along tonight when my dad drives us to the dance. I think she can hardly believe I have a date; she wants to see for herself. Don't be surprised if she pokes you, to be sure you're real."

"That wouldn't surprise me at all." I smiled at him. "I don't mind if they both come. My mom will probably make you all come in so she can take a couple thousand pictures."

"Parents." He shrugged. "Mine have just spotted me. I see my mom crying and running at the same time. I better go head her off before she trips over a child or a chair. Congratulations on your award, and don't forget, the whole Family Flink will be at your door by seven sharp!"

"I'll be ready! Thanks . . . for everything."

"No prob."

I watched him hug his mom and dad.

Then my mom found me. "Oh, honey, I'm so proud of you! Let me see your award!"

"Me too, me too!" said Kate. "Cyril knew you were a winner, Melia! He always said so! Watch out, Cyril. I know you want to see, but you're standing on my toe!"

"Isn't it beautiful, Mom? And look, Richard made me a little jewelry box." I handed my treasures to her. "I want to get a little silver chain for the medal right away, so I can wear it. You know, when Mr. Christopher called my name I was so shocked, I nearly dropped dead!"

"I'm so pleased that you didn't do that!" Mr. Christopher said with a laugh as he appeared behind Mom. "I just polished these shoes. No telling what a dead body would have done to the shine."

"Oh, hi, Mr. C. This is my mom and my little sister, Kate."

"I'm Frances Fleeman." Mom took his hand. "It's so good to meet you. Amelia talks about you constantly.

"That's good, I hope," he said.

"Oh, yes it is," said Kate. "She had a crush on you last year. I'm pretty sure."

"Now, Kate," said Mom quickly. "Don't be silly. You'll embarrass your sister."

"Too late," I said.

"That's perfectly understandable. Why, everyone has a crush on me! It's a rule at our school!"

"Really?" said wide-eyed Kate.

I looked gratefully at him and poked her. "Come on, Kate, let's go find Shura and give her our present." I grabbed my award and Shura's gift out of Mom's purse. "We'll be back in a flash, Mom!"

"I'll wait by the refreshment table," she called.

"So will I," called Mr. Christopher.

We found Shura outside with her family. Mr. Najinsky looked antsy, and Rudy, her little brother was already waiting in the car.

"Hi, Mr. and Mrs. Najinsky," I said.

"Hi, too," said Kate.

"Hello, girls. What a nice award for you, my dear Amelia," said Mrs. Najinsky. "You have been deserving, I am sure."

Mr. Najinsky coughed. "Yes, veddy nice. You girls say good-bye now. We must be getting on our way to airport."

"Okay, Pop," said Shura. "I'm comin' in a sec." She hugged me. "Hey, pal! You are the BFD of the day! I'm so proud of you! You deserve that award. You really put your heart and soul into that place. Let's have a look."

"Thanks, Shur. Isn't it pretty?"

"It's beautiful, Amelia. Really artistic."

Wendy floated up to us. "I've been looking all over for you!" She was wearing an off-the-shoulder, white tunic, goddess thing. "What a nice prize," she said. "Can I look at it next?"

"Sure." I handed it to her.

"I really envy you, Amelia. Your award is the only really special one they gave out."

"Gee, thanks, Wendy. Thanks a lot."

"I have to run, my dad is waiting, and he hates to be kept waiting. I've still got to get my hair done and my nails wrapped, all before the dance tonight! I have to look pretty for Bill!" She flipped her hair back and smiled. "Well, send me a postcard from Russia, Shura! And Amelia, maybe I'll see you at the pool this summer!"

"Maybe! See ya."

I watched the Mustang screech away.

"Shura, Shura, look what we got you. Look! Look!" Kate jumped around under her nose. "It's a going away, graduation present."

"Wow! You guys shouldn't have bought me anything!"

"Why not?" asked Kate.

"Yeah, you're right, Katrinka, why not? I deserve a present!" She ripped into the paper and opened the box. "Oh, I love them, thank you so much!"

It was a set of nice paint brushes in a carrying case.

"Hey, when Amelia is a famous actress, I'll paint her portrait with these!"

"Goody!" said Kate. "And you can paint me right now! This is my best dress. I wore it special."

"Not right away, Kate. We'll be gone all summer. I'll have to paint you in the fall."

"Okay. I'll still be here! Melia, I'm going over there by that tree. I see Trisha, from my school. She invited me to come and play at her house this summer."

"Okay, but stay by the tree where I can find you."

I turned to Shura. "I guess I have to say good-bye here, don't I?"

"And I have to say dah sveedahneeyah. I better make the switch to my mother tongue."

"It sounds perfect to me. Sad, but perfect." We hugged.

"I'll miss you," I said. "Write to me. It's going to be another long, hot summer."

"You write, too. Tell me about Flinky and the big dance. Maybe I'll meet a tall, mysterious Russian guy and bring him back as an exchange student!"

"*That* would be exciting!"

"My mother would be thrilled. Well, my pop is straining at the car keys over there. I'll write to you on the plane!"

"I'll write tonight, after the dance!"

I waved until they drove away, then I got Kate, and went back to Mom and Mr. C.

"Oh, Noel, that is the funniest story!" Mom was laughing and wiping her eyes.

"Mommy! I'm so hungry, can we go eat now?" asked Kate.

"Noel, the girls and I are going out to have a celebration lunch. I don't suppose you'd be free?"

"As a bird!" he said. "I'm as free as they come, Frances. How about you?"

"It just so happens that I'm free, too."

He grinned. "Then that makes four of us, right Amelia?"

I fingered my talisman. "Yep. That's right, Mr. C. That makes four of us! Time to spread our wings!"

We got in the car and headed for my favorite Chinese restaurant.

"I was thinking . . ." I said.

"Always a good sign!" said Mr. C.

"Har, har! Anyway, I was thinking it would be good to have a summer program at Bret Harte. The kids have often complained to me how bored they are in the summer. Don't you think they need something?"

"It's funny you should say that. Just this morning, I was talking to Ruth Weiss, our English teacher, about starting a summer program for the kids. Not so much academics, more like a summer camp."

"That's what I meant, too! I thought we could have dramatics and put on a play!"

"I heard of a school in San Francisco that does that every year. I could call them and ask for details."

"Summer is usually so dull, I bet lots of kids from my school would volunteer."

"I would!" said Kate. "I'd like to help."

"We'd love to have your help, Kate. We need bright kids, like you and your sister." He smiled from the front seat.

"I have lots of ideas!" I bubbled enthusiastically. "My friend, Richard, he loves to read plays. I bet we could get him to direct it!"

"This is fabulous!" said Mr. Christopher. "Let's make some definite plans over lunch."

"You know what?" said Mom. "I could teach a first-aid class to the kids. If you think anyone would sign up?"

"Wow!" Mr. C. laughed. "Did I hit the jackpot with this family, or what?"

Mom smiled. She and Mr. C. started talking about Mom's work.

I sighed happily and leaned back to read my yearbook. People always write such goofy stuff in yearbooks, but it was nice to have a memento.

I flipped around, reading and chuckling. A lot of

kids made jokes about seeing me on the Candy Crowley show. I stopped on the page that had my picture. Someone had signed right near my face with quite a flair and a flourish. I looked closely.

"To Amelia, that nice, quiet, girl. Who really is never all alone! Fondly, Lily."

I didn't know anyone named Lily.

Did I?

Oh well, maybe I just forgot. I shook my head and closed the book on my Highland Grade School days.

As we drove, I glanced out the window. There, sitting on a bus that was driving along right next to us, was the same beautiful lady in white I had seen in the greenroom of the Candy K. Crowley show.

She waved. I waved back.

I noticed something else. On the side of the bus, just beneath her, was an advertisement for Celestial Seasonings Herb Teas.

They had a new flavor, Angelic Amaretto.

I felt a tingle go up my spine. Was somebody trying to tell me something?

Four Wondrous Stories
of Adventure and Courage by
B R I A N
J A C Q U E S

70828-0/$4.99 US

70827-2/$4.99 US

MATTIMEO

71530-9/$4.99 US

MARIEL OF REDWALL

71922-3/$4.99 US